JASON AS A
YOUNG BOY

JASON AS A YOUNG BOY

A NOVEL

Wolfgang Schoellkopf

ARBOR BOOKS, INC

Cover design by Henry M. Doster
hankdoster@comcast.net

Book design by:
Arbor Books, Inc.
www.arborbooks.com

Printed in the United States of America

Jason As a Young Boy
Wolfgang Schoellkopf

1. Title 2. Author 3. Fiction

Library of Congress Control Number: 2012946257

ISBN: 978-0-9841992-6-6

Jason, be advised
games aren't life
to be is to do

Table of Contents

Prolegomena 1

Nautika 25

Medeia 85

Epilogos 121

PROLEGOMENA

The Hellenes call me Cheiron, the old man of the mountain. Many years ago, when my hair was black and my limbs were strong, I felt a need for solitude, time and space away from the school where I taught the children of the people who had grabbed our land and exiled us to Pelion. Life on the mountain is hell, a warren of hills and ravines, millions of silent trees, ravaged by anabatic winds. Pelion's inaccessibility protects our liberty, but it comes at a heavy price. Without an inch of arable land, we cannot grow barley; without grazing land, we cannot raise cattle. Centuries ago we brought the art of farming to these lands; now we herd goats, hunt rabbits and boars, and scrounge for food in the forest. Worst of all is coping to live without hope, mind and soul compelled to accept a degraded life, helplessly resigned to a world ruled by others.

With life on Pelion being difficult enough, my personal situation brought added frustration and pain. Still single at nineteen, I faced the prospect of having to wait another ten years before Chariklo could be mine—sweet Chariklo, love of my dreams. Philyra, my mother, mocked me for falling in love with a five-year-old girl, insisting I wait until she reached her fifteenth year. Although prepared to forbear, I needed assurance that my dream would come true in time, which meant I had to ask for Chariklo's parents' consent. Yet fear of rebuff, and a faintness of heart, prevented me from seeking permission. Philyra called me a fool, and I guess I was. My hesitation morphed into dejection; no one felt my pain or understood my dubiety, making each day worse than the one before. I had to escape this trap of mind. The way out was to get off the mountain, sort out my thinking, and, so I hoped, keep my depression at bay.

And that was what I did. Early one morning, when dawn had cleared the stars from the pale sky, I threw caution to the wind and clambered down Pelion's steep slopes, slowly at first but faster as cliffs and ravines gave way to more gradual terrain nearer the shore of Pagasae Bay. I well remember the day: it was a beautiful September morning, balmy rather than hot, my heart beating at a steady pace, calming my restless mind. Reaching the shore of the bay, I plunged headfirst into the water, swimming toward distant Iolkos until my arms grew heavy from the unaccustomed exercise. I had been to Iolkos once before, but the Minyans there had made fun of me, laughing at my hairy chest and dark-toned skin and calling me half man, half horse. While I couldn't have cared less about the Minyans or any other Hellene, their nasty baiting and foul-mouthed threats taught me never to visit their town again.

Turning around I slowly swam back toward the shore, stood when my feet touched ground, and waded across the pebble-strewn beach, careful not to wrench an ankle or bruise a toe. My descent down the mountain had left me more tired than I cared to admit, my lungs gasping for air, legs feeling like bags of sand. Why not stay another day? Why rush home? I asked myself. Why not extend my sojourn a while? The deserted shore seemed perfectly safe for spending the night.

Weighing the thought in my mind while treading across the stony beach, I was shocked to the core when a horse-drawn wagon pulled up a mere twenty paces ahead. It was a well-made conveyance, five or six yards in length, equipped with four-spoke, wooden wheels and pulled by two small horses. For an instant my brain couldn't process what my eyes beheld. I'd believed I was alone—suddenly I was not! I thought I was safe, but now faced disaster. This was a Minyan wagon: I would be captured, I would be enslaved. My doom was sealed!

Dumbfounded and deeply alarmed, I halted my stride and retreated a step as a tall, blond-haired Minyan jumped off the driver's bench, eying me in an arrogant albeit strangely questioning way. His very size frightened me, and my apprehension turned to cold panic when I noticed a second person sitting on the wagon's bench. Facing one enemy might have left me with half a chance, but I couldn't possibly prevail against two. How careless, how stupid of me to get caught by two marauders of the master race! No wonder we'd lost our land first to the filthy Pelasgi and then to the vainglorious Hellenes. My father and my father's father had taught me everything there was to know except how to escape while standing naked in knee-deep water.

Yet my fear proved groundless—completely so. For presently the tall Hellene opened his cloak, showing me he bore no arms. He sported a full beard except for his shaved upper lip; he was clad in a belt-girded chiton and an ornate purple cloak, and his feet were sheathed in elaborate sandals. Rings adorned his hands, and a golden chain circled his neck. This was no ordinary Hellene. This man was a nobleman!

To my utter surprise, he extended his right hand and

addressed me by my given name: "The gods be with you, Cheiron. I fervently hope you are who I say."

"Yes, my lord, they call me Cheiron."

"I am Aeson, son of Kretheos, and sitting in the wagon is Alkimede, my beloved wife."

"Cheiron is honored by your presence."

"Thanks be to deathless Zeus for guiding us to you. We have traveled for days on end, up and down these shores, hoping to find you and benefit from your advice."

So this was the reclusive Aeson, the much talked about but seldom seen Minyan prince, the half brother of King Peleas; they shared the same mother but sprang from different fathers. When Aeson began to speak, Alkimede climbed off the wagon to stand next to her husband. She was beautifully dressed in an ankle-length gown with a close-fitting bodice and a wide-flouncing skirt girt at the waist. An exquisite necklace and sandals with upturned toes completed her regal appearance.

Aeson spoke in an eloquent, graceful manner, yet what he said was old hat—stories well known throughout Thessaly. I couldn't care less who ruled the Minyans, whether it was Peleas, Aeson, or their almighty Zeus. To me all Hellenes were equally despicable—invaders who had taken our land and enslaved our people except for the few who had managed to escape into the thicket of Pelion. Yet here was the king's brother staring at my black hair and my olive skin, knowing nothing about our thousand-year culture, our homeland in the distant East, or the golden age when we grew barley and emmer and raised livestock in the fertile Thessalian plain. For all I knew, Aeson believed he was descended from one of their gods, but surely he wasn't divine, only powerful and wealthy while I had only myself.

What arrogance to claim descent from a god! The Hellenes

are the only people on earth who believe that in appearance and disposition the gods are like them and they are like gods. The only differences between a Hellene and his gods are that the gods don't die and are super strong. What a simplistic religion! Seemingly fixated on power and immortality, the Hellenes are smart enough to know they have neither, and straightaway they invent gods who possess these exact attributes. Knowing what one wishes to have doesn't mean it in fact exists. Yet the Hellenes not only believe their gods are real; they believe they are the gods' descendants and therefore blessed with superior genes that place the Hellenic race above the rest of humanity, above people like us. While there's no material evidence for any of this, the Hellenic religion confers on the believer amazing self-confidence, a belief of being morally superior, and an inherent right to rule the world. Yet there I stood, facing not just any Hellene but the arrogantly self-confident brother of a king. What could this powerful prince possibly want from lowly me?

Well, Aeson didn't say—not at first and not for a long while. He talked about Peleas and Tyro, his power-hungry brother and their perfidious mother, and how his family had been founded by Aiolos, who had conquered this land by driving out the Pelasgian scum. Aeson asserted that his people had never made war against us—that the Hellenes and my people were friends sharing the same beautiful country according to our respective traditions, they cultivating the plain and we living on the mountain. I wasn't sure whether Aeson took me for a fool or actually believed Minyan rule was the natural order of things, a world designed, no doubt, by Zeus himself, who, so they say, not only likes to have his way with women but also with little boys.

Aware of my puzzled countenance, Alkimede stepped

forward and, speaking in an uncertain voice, said how help-less newborn babies are. Babies? What babies? What was she talking about? Her words didn't connect, made no sense at all, and I must have looked oddly perplexed when I quickly agreed that what she said was true. Yes, newborns can do nothing for themselves; by nature's norm their births are premature. If they aren't fed, kept warm, cleaned and cuddled, they cannot thrive and surely will die. On hearing the word *die*, Alkimede started to cry, buried her head in her husband's arms and, with tears streaming from her eyes, shouted she wanted her baby to live. Now my puzzlement was complete. What child? And why was the princess in such distress?

Confusion clouded my brow. Aeson placed his hand on my shoulder, saying we needed to talk man to man or, better still, converse like old friends—in his language, of course. He said we should talk as if we were working in the fields together or having supper at his house. What a preposterous notion! The king's brother having supper with me was so far beyond the realm of the possible it had no meaning at all. What was this all about?

Aeson claimed he wanted to talk, but then barely said any-thing of consequence. Why didn't he explain what he wanted instead of beating around the bush? Why in the name of Zeus had he and his wife looked for me on the shore of Pagasae Bay? But Aeson took his time, droning on about his grand-father Aiolos and his many sons. One was Kretheos, Aeson's father; another was Salmoneus, the father of Tyro, who was Aeson's mother, which meant his father was also his mother's uncle. However, before his parents were married, his mother had borne two sons by Enipeus, called Peleas and Neleus. The trouble arose when Tyro chose Peleas rather than Aeson as king.

Aeson said he was without political ambition and professed to have conceded the throne to his brother willingly. Peleas had accepted Aeson's compliant abdication but nonetheless lived in constant fear that other members of the family may come to challenge his kingship on grounds of his illegitimate birth. Peleas's phobia had become a metastasizing cancer, the king suspecting each and every member of the royal family and decreeing that baby boys born to a prince had to be exposed to the elements and left to die. And this, said Aeson, was the reason why they came to see me.

"My Lord, I don't understand!"

"Cheiron, don't you see? We want our son to live!"

"You have a son? Where is he?"

"He's asleep in the wagon, unaware of his uncertain fate."

Alkimede reached into the wagon and carefully retrieved a small bundle wrapped in swaddling clothes. Pushing back an edge of the finely woven fabric, she uncovered the face of a very young baby, no more than three or four weeks old. She said no one knew of the child's existence: she had assiduously concealed her pregnancy, secretly delivered the baby at their hunting lodge, and kept the little boy hidden in their private rooms behind the megaron. Yet with each passing day the chance of discovery grew. Servants were bustling all over the palace, visitors came and had to be entertained, and at night friends would join Aeson for dinner and conversation. Sooner or later someone was bound to hear or see the baby, and a favor-seeking scoundrel would betray their little boy to Peleas.

They had named the baby Diomedes, which meant *cunning* in the Hellenic tongue, knowing full well that the child's life depended on cunning and luck. Yet cunning and luck were not enough; the odds of discovery were not in their baby's favor. Despite all their precautions, they could not assure the boy's safety as long as he lived with them. The only way to assure his survival was for him to have different parents and a new name. Alkimede confirmed that the purpose of their travel to the eastern shore of Pagasae Bay was to find a new home for their dear son, preferably on Pelion and preferably with me because I taught school and was known as a healer. My reward for raising and teaching Diomedes until his twentieth year would be ten sheep per year—on the condition that I would never reveal the boy's royal lineage.

Ten sheep per year for twenty years meant lots of meat and plenty of fleece for our poor. After decades of deprivation and meager food, Aeson's offer was like a gift from heaven. But could I trust this gift-bearing Hellene to honor his end of the bargain? What if I accepted the baby but never got a single sheep? Everyone knew that the Hellenes were habitual liars who were actually proud of their skills in deception and ruse. Since Aeson was a Hellene, it seemed only logical to assume that he too was a liar. But was it correct to judge him this way? Wasn't he defying Peleas at the risk of his own life? It made no sense for him to deceive me on that day.

But would Aeson keep his promise five, ten, or fifteen years from then? Would he deliver ten sheep year after year for twenty years? I was at loss for an answer until I put myself in Aeson' place and considered how he saw me. Aeson, being Hellenic, would have seen me as half man, half horse, a brutish barbarian without scruples or conscience. While he was unable to trust his fellow Minyans, Aeson chose me not because he liked me but because he saw me as the least objectionable of all the people on Pelion. In his eyes I was a barbarian—uncouth, amoral, and without honor, more animal than man, and one he would fully expect to kill his child if he, Aeson, were to violate the terms of our deal. So, paradoxical as it seemed, I decided to trust him precisely because he thought so little of me.

I was also swayed by Aeson and Alkimede themselves. They looked and talked like Minyans but without the arrogant swagger of their Iolkos compatriots. They neither threatened me nor boasted about their royal descent, and the more we talked the more their Hellenic-ness receded, revealing them at their core as two loving parents trying to save their son. The more we talked, the less foreign they seemed, and so, casting aside my misgivings, I agreed to care for the boy as long as Aeson would deliver ten sheep every year. Mind you all this occurred many years before the wedding feast of Peirithoos. Had I known then what would happen later, there would have been no adoption, not at any price.

Before formally accepting the boy, I asked to examine his limbs, measure his pulse, and feel the strength of his breath. Life on Pelion was harsh, and there was no point in taking the baby up the mountain if he was sickly or weak. So Aeson spread a blanket on the ground, and Alkimede tenderly opened the baby's clothes. She kissed his forehead and his soft belly while I felt his arms and legs and laid my hand on his gently heaving chest. The boy was healthy and hale! He had blue eyes and a wisp of blond hair, and his skin was fair except for two little red spots, one on his left foot and the other on his right thigh. Alkimede hadn't noticed them before, and they looked harmless indeed.

So I nodded my head, Aeson shook my hand, and Alkimede started to weep. We discussed my journey back up the mountain and decided Alkimede should nurse her baby for the last time. She pushed aside her chiton, and little Diomedes put his mouth to his mother's roseate nipple and eagerly started to suck. When he slowed and then stopped, Alkimede offered him her other breast, and Diomedes resumed drinking his mother's milk, all the while kicking his legs in consummate pleasure. She then held the baby on her shoulder, gently patting his back until he burped and burped again. Then it was time to say good-bye.

Aeson folded a long piece of cloth into a sling around my neck, and Alkimede ever so gently placed Diomedes into it, then covered the baby with a purple cloth. The air was still, the leaves without voice, the only sound coming from wavelets lapping against the pebbles covering the beach. Father and mother stood motionless and utterly silent, their eyes fixed on the bundle holding their son. I turned and quickly strode into the underbrush, aware that I would be climbing all night before reaching the cave and finding a wet nurse to nourish my entrusted charge. The distance from the beach to my place was about thirty miles and a full fifteen hundred feet above Pagasae Bay. Setting out at four in the afternoon, I figured it would take nine hours to get home—a long time for the baby to be without food and having to depend solely on the honey-sweetened water that filled my leather bottle.

The first five miles were easy, and I made good time. The terrain was uphill but not overly steep, and the little boy was soundly asleep. But then the going got tough. Not only did the mountain's gradient steepen with every step, but the goat track I followed was too narrow for the boy and me. And it was pitch-dark, with the sun blocked out and the moon only a faint sliver of light.

After three hours of steady climbing, I needed to rest and catch my breath, but when I halted my step Diomedes started to bawl. Used to the sway of my gait, the boy reacted to the cessation of motion and began to protest as loudly as his little voice could. Earthquakes may open the ground and lightning can split the sky, but nothing is more powerful than a baby's cry. Not knowing what bothered the little bugger, or why or where, I quickly resumed climbing in order to stop his vociferous protestation. While his parents had chosen me to teach him, the baby wasted no time in turning the tables, instructing me to hurry up and find a full-breasted nanny to serve him breakfast and lunch. So I climbed all night without attempting another stop other than hiding Alkimede's purple cloth behind a rock. Each time the baby started to whimper or otherwise fuss, I pressed the leather bottle's nozzle against his lips, and the honey-flavored water calmed him a bit. I reached my mountain cave well after midnight and immediately roused Hagno, the wet nurse, to give Diomedes his first meal on Pelion.

With the baby sated and his diaper changed, I took him to Philyra, dissimulating that I had found him exposed on the beach. Mother sadly shook her head, calling the Hellenes a cruel race, the only people on earth who would expose a baby they considered imperfect or otherwise didn't want. Unfolding the swaddling sheets, Philyra closely examined Diomedes and, pleasantly surprised, exclaimed how strong and healthy he was. She called him a beautiful boy, well-nourished and mentally alert, and failed to understand why any parent would expose such a perfectly formed child. Philyra noticed only one irregularity, namely the small, reddish spots on his left foot and upper right thigh. The redness was slightly raised, and Philyra tried to suck out whatever poison might have been under the skin. She believed the spots were tick bites and hoped her suction would remove the poison. I thought the spots were too small to be bites, and quickly dismissed her concern.

Philyra was nothing but practical. The baby needed a bed and a place to live, and she decided he would sleep next to her and live in her part of the cave. She asked a neighbor, Pholos, to build a wooden crib draped with soft fleece for comfort and warmth; she told Hagno the times to feed him; and she assigned me the task of telling the boy a new story every night. The previous day Diomedes had been the son of a Minyan prince; within a day of his arrival on Pelion he had acquired a new mother, healthy food, a comfortable bed, and a safe abode. He had become one of us in spite of his Minyan blood.

Henceforth Diomedes would live our life and absorb our customs while I would cram him full of facts and teach him how to reason. But I would speak to him only in Hellenic, and so would Philyra and Hagno and anyone else he would meet on the mountain. To live successfully in the current world, Diomedes had to speak the Hellenic language accent-free. Even back then I knew that the future belonged to the Hellenes, not to us, and that Diomedes would have to live his adult life in the Hellenic world. But teaching him only Hellenic was not going to be without cost. Since language provides the mind with its conceptual grid, speaking Hellenic would mean that the boy would be thinking as a Hellene. I would teach him how to reason, but he would think like a Hellene, not like one of us.

On the fifteenth day of October, I walked twenty-one miles to a place near the pastures of the Hellenes and collected the ten sheep Aeson had promised. What Aeson didn't know was that his payment had become entirely redundant the moment I had adopted his son. Diomedes, small and helpless as he was, had captured my heart. I felt like a cheat taking Aeson's sheep when in truth I would have gladly paid him for the gift of his son.

But my scruples promptly dissolved into thin air when I reminded myself of our people's nagging poverty. Basic needs command priority; morality comes second. I took the sheep because we needed them, and I took care of Diomedes because I loved him. Yet the more I loved Diomedes the more I disliked his theophorous name. And so, until a more fitting eponym came to mind, I simply called him "boy."

Everyone on Pelion loved the boy, and everyone wanted to know where I had found him and who he was. But with ten sheep each year for twenty years at stake, I was never going to tell anyone, not even Philyra, who he was or how his parents had found me. I had one simple story for all ears and avoided elaborating for fear of contradicting myself. For a lie to hold up and be accepted as true, it must be straightforward and simple, without codicils and marginalia that are prone to expose the liar. So I promised myself to lie no more than required to protect the boy.

My story was that I'd found him on Pagasae Bay, wrapped in swaddling clothes and a purple cloak. But where was the purple cloak? Well, I'd lost it on the way up; it was pitch dark, I stumbled, and then it was gone. Everyone heard the same story, and the questions eventually stopped.

When the boy turned one, he started to walk, assert his will, and act with intent, aware of the difference between him and others. When he was two, he said *mi, pa, gala, artos, skylos, ornis,* and another thirty or so words, but only when Philyra, his *mi,* was around. When he was three, he wanted to be like his *mi* and his *pa,* drank lots of milk and ate bread by the loaf, played with the puppy, and endlessly watched birds flying hither and thither. When he was four, he realized he was a boy and started to mimic me and other males around the cave. And, at pace with his mental development, his arms and legs grew strong and sturdy, blond curls framed his handsome face, and his clear eyes were always curious and alert. We had the perfect child, or so it seemed.

I saw the boy mostly in the evening, after I returned from teaching at the school. We would have supper together, and after Philyra put him to bed it was my task to tell him a new story every night. As I had never liked the Hellenic gods and was more or less convinced they didn't exist, my nightly narrations focused on stories about historical persons—men who had slain beasts and dragons, showed courage in battle, traveled the oceans, or founded new cities. Soon the boy knew everything there was to know about Bellerophon, Daidalos, Danaos, Kadmos, Pelops, Perseus, Phoroneus, Phrixos, and even young Herakles, who had graduated from our school only two years before. Of the stories I rendered, some true and others mere fables, the boy's favorites were about Danaos sailing up from Egypt, Kadmos coming to Thebes, Pelops travelling from Lydia to Pisa, and Phrixos leaving for Kolchis, never to return. The boy would listen raptly, remembering every nuance of every tale, and at only four years old he knew more history than my pupils at the school.

But then everything changed. At five the boy's interest noticeably flagged. He often seemed bored, restless, and impatient. Strange twitches crisscrossed his face, occasionally at first but then with alarming frequency. And the boy threw tantrums, whether in pain or out of frustration we didn't know. No one symptom was virulent by itself, but when we saw them in conjunction and growing in number, we realized something was terribly wrong.

The boy's earlier distinct enunciation turned into a slur, making his speech close to incomprehensible. His formerly firm gait became awkward and clumsy, while his eye and hand coordination degenerated to a point where he couldn't throw a stone or catch a ball. Philyra mothered the boy in all possible ways, taking him on long walks through the forest and stuffing him with nutritious meals. And her efforts did meet with some success. The boy was tall for his age, his wide shoulders gave his arms maximum space, and his straight back lent him perfect posture. But whenever he moved—walked, ran, or grasped an object—he was oddly uncoordinated, his hands, arms, and legs seeming to move in different directions.

Philyra was deeply upset. Her little darling was beautiful and strong, and she did her best to make him so, yet it was obvious that he was desperately ill. In desperation Philyra experimented with the boy's diet, thinking he might be allergic to one food or another. At first she limited his meals to vegetables only and then went the opposite way by feeding him venison and lamb, and when the all-protein diet had no effect she tried dairy-free for a while, and finally settled on fruit juice and gruel, which the boy refused to eat. Regardless of what he ate, his condition grew progressively worse, with no one knowing its nature or cause. My father had taught me all the medicine known to man, yet I had no clue what was happening to the boy. Philyra was furious: Wasn't I the know-it-all doctor? Hadn't I cured hundreds of people, some of them heroes and kings? But what good was my knowledge when I couldn't help my own son?

Lacking a diagnosis, I resolved to reconstruct the boy's medical history since the day he was born. From the time of his beachfront adoption, I had been with him every single day. He had the flu a few times, but with the help of borage he always recovered quickly. He had stomachaches every so often but, when treated with thyme, never for more than a couple of days. He had never been seriously ill, nor bodily injured, nor had he ever been bitten by an animal, domesticated or wild.

The only time I hadn't been with him was during his first twenty days, when his natural parents had concealed him in their lodge at the foot of the Olympos Massive, an area useless for farming, but where the Hellenes hunted boar and deer.

Did I say deer? Yes, of course, there would have been deer at Aeson's hunting lodge, and deer are not as cute and innocent as they seem. When Philyra had examined the boy on his arrival, she'd noticed two tiny, red spots and thought they were deer-tick bites. But, never having seen any ticks on the mountain, I'd brushed aside her concern. Indeed the spots disappeared, and that seemed the end of that. But perhaps I was wrong. Perhaps the boy had been bitten before I'd adopted him. There could have been ticks around the hunting lodge where his parents hid him during the first weeks of his life. If so the ticks' poison would have been in his blood for too many years. Could tick bites account for his awkward speech and irascible temper? In truth, I didn't know. I was familiar with herbs and their healing power, but had no idea what happened to blood when infected by an animal toxin.

Crotchety old Nessos, however, knew more about blood than anyone on the mountain. When I told Philyra about asking him for advice, she strongly objected, calling Nessos a quarrelsome, vindictive scoundrel who hated the Hellenes and therefore could not be trusted with the boy's life. But I needed to know about blood, and since Nessos was an expert on blood I asked Gryneios to bring him to me.

When I described the boy's condition, Nessos immediately suggested the boy may have been bitten by ticks. Nessos explained that ticks put poison into the blood, and since blood was everywhere in the body—chest, belly, legs, arms, and head—the poison could affect any and all parts. But what was this poison that ticks put into human blood? Was it a curse or magic or what?

Nessos laughed, saying there were no such things as curses or magic. Poison was poison, a harmful substance, but without knowing what kind of poison we were dealing with we had no basis for treatment. Nessos thought there was a way to find out what was in the boy's blood, but it had not been tried before. If we knew the poison's nature—inert or alive—we might have a fighting chance to cure the disease.

"Nessos, what are you talking about? How can we possibly know what poison is inside the boy?"

"We examine a drop of his blood."

"Examine it how? Taste it or smell it or feel its stickiness?"

"No, Cheiron, nothing of the sort. We examine the boy's blood by looking at it through a piece of curved glass."

"Oh, you mean the glass pieces our people brought from the East."

"Yes, that's what I mean. Viewing an object through one of the glasses magnifies its size. Do you still have any of them?"

"I have five or six."

"Good. I own four. Let's take a look and select the best— the one that magnifies the most."

And that was what we did. We tested each curved glass by viewing a strand of hair through it. The thicker the hair's appearance under the glass, the greater was the glass's magnification. Soon we had selected the best.

Next was to get a drop of blood from the boy who, at that

time, was eating supper with Philyra and Hagno. We explained our need, but the women adamantly refused—as I'd known they would—to cut the boy's finger for a drop of his blood. Philyra didn't trust Nessos and didn't believe a word he said, and Hagno agreed with whatever Philyra said.

But Nessos didn't give up. He patiently explained the reasons for what we had to do. After an hour or so, the boy went to bed, and Philyra burst out, "Okay. Go ahead and do it, but do it fast."

So I took my sharpest knife and made a small cut at the tip of the boy's right-hand middle finger. He screamed, but we had his *dara*, and we immediately examined the reddish fluid under the glass we had picked.

Nessos was first to speak: "Cheiron, bad luck: the poison in the boy's blood is alive."

"How do you know?"

"Look closely and you will see little, spiral-shaped things moving about. They shouldn't be there, and they shouldn't move, but since they are moving we know they are alive."

"But why is this bad luck?"

"To cure the boy, we have to kill the spirals without killing the boy."

Looking sad and deflated, Nessos didn't know what we could possibly do. I suggested consulting Asbolos and Dryas, or going to Iolkos to see a Hellenic doctor. But Nessos shook his head, saying there was no treatment for live poison in the blood. No one, he said, knew a cure for the illness; indeed, he claimed, it was impossible to treat any illness, or any patient for that matter, that lacked a name. Treatment had to be based on fact and reason, but the mind can't deal with a thing that has no name.

So, the first thing we had to do, Nessos insisted, was to

give names not only to the boy's illness but also to the patient himself. Nessos suggested *tick disease* for the illness and challenged me to name the boy. His parents had called him Diomedes, and yet, surely, the boy's *deos* had done nothing to prevent those ticks from poisoning his blood. The boy needed a cure, not a useless god, so I proposed to call him *Iasis*, which was what he needed. Philyra liked the idea but not the Hellenic word, and insisted his name should be Jason instead.

Having named the patient and his disease, we still needed a name for the poison. Kroronos happened to pay Philyra a visit that day and, joining our discussion, inquired what we were talking about. Nessos explained that the cause of Jason's illness was a tiny, spiral-shaped staff, what the Hellenes called a *bakterion*. Kroronos laughed, asking why we were scratching our heads for a word when the thing already had a name. And didn't it make sense to give Jason's poison a Hellenic name since the spirals were enemies like the Hellenes, enemies we wanted to kill?

Nessos clapped his hands in approval, calling *bacteria*—as he mispronounced the word—a perfect name for the spirally devils. I know all this sounds a bit crazy, but that was how we felt at the time.

Yet we still didn't know how the bacteria made Jason sick. The spirals lived in the blood and had to eat to stay alive, ingesting either the blood they lived in or other parts of the body. My hunch was the bacteria weren't eating blood but tissue, somehow consuming tiny snips of the boy's heart, clips of his liver, or gobs of his brain. One way to kill the spirals was to starve them to death, but since Jason needed his heart, liver, and brain to live, we needed an alternative therapy that would cure him without killing his organs. The question was: why had Jason's blood harbored the deer-tick bacteria while the blood of others did not?

Nessos wasn't keen about my line of reasoning but readily admitted that some people's blood was stronger than others, and that people with weak blood were often sick. Well, was there a way to make Jason's weak blood strong? Nessos laughed, saying Jason would have to drink lots of colostrum, the milk of she-goats in the first two days after giving birth to a kid. Colostrum, Nessos explained, was a thick, yellowish fluid that fought off diseases afflicting newborn goats. He thought we should give it a try, and so did I. With hundreds of goats roaming Pelion, colostrum was easy to find and collect.

Philyra, thank goodness, somehow persuaded Jason to drink the icky stuff and, lo and behold, after six months of imbibing gallons of the sticky brew, he rarely suffered spasms, his headaches were gone, and his tantrums became things of the past. But while Jason was no longer violently sick, we found, to our dismay, that the spirals had damaged his body and impaired his functionality. He spoke only haltingly and was unable to recall many words; he had trouble adding and subtracting numbers, and he couldn't remember a story a minute after hearing it. Now we knew that what we'd feared was true: while the colostrum had killed the bacteria quickly enough, Jason's organs had been damaged before the colostrum had a chance to do its work. This was very bad news. Everyone on the mountain had hoped that Jason would someday be able to lead a normal life, but now all bets were off.

The day came when Jason turned ten. We threw him a big party; everyone laughed and had fun, but many of Jason's old friends seemed reluctant to join in. Aware that Jason had been ill for a long time, none of the children mocked or abused him.

However his halting speech and physical clumsiness set him apart, his impairments erecting an invisible wall between him and his childhood friends. Jason stood in the room's left corner, watching his birthday guests play games and sing merry songs while he was unable to participate. When the party was over, he flopped on his bed and sobbed inconsolably. Philyra was deeply upset, crying long into the night and finding it hard to accept that colostrum had done wonders killing the spirals but proved useless in restoring Jason to health.

At my wit's end, I decided to visit Kroronos, who was justly famous for his common sense, and ask his advice in the hope that he would see what I had missed.

"Kroronos, what are we to do? Jason's still sick!"

"You are wrong. Jason isn't sick. He is merely disabled."

"Krorones, please! Don't make fun of Jason's disease."

"Cheiron, I am serious. Your treatment worked, and the bacteria are gone, which means Jason is no longer sick. The reason Jason is clumsy and slow, the reason his speech is impaired, is that the spirals damaged his muscles and nerves. Jason isn't sick. He is disabled. His body has to relearn what the bacteria destroyed. He requires instruction on how to move his arms and legs and how to speak and think."

"But, Kroronos, teaching can't restore what's no longer there."

"We don't know what was destroyed and what remains, but we know the body can be trained to perform new tasks and learn by repetition. Make his arm throw a spear until he does it right. Make his tongue and lips say words until they sound as they should. Endless repetition is the way for Jason's body to recover what it lost."

"Perhaps you are right—physical exercises may help. But what about his mind, his slow thought?"

"The mind is part of the body, which means you do the same thing: instruction and practice, endlessly repeated, until Jason's mind performs the way it should."

Kroronos made intuitive sense, and on the hike back to the cave I racked my brain about how best to implement his advice. If an arm forgot how to throw a stone, then that arm must relearn through practice until its muscles can execute a perfect motion. I would ask Jason to throw various-sized stones across the ravine and hit specified targets on the other side. And I would put him through drills in running, climbing, swimming, wrestling, and handling a sword, all the time relentlessly training his body until every intended physical movement became second nature to him. Kroronos was right. Repetitive exercise was the way to go, and I was determined to train Jason's body back to perfection.

But what about Jason's mind? The mind isn't muscles, tendons, and nerves, but something weightless and invisible. No one knows where the mind is—some think it's in the heart, others in the liver or brain—and no one knows how the mind thinks and how it gets to know what it knows. Babies are born with instincts—crying when in pain, suckling when hungry—and an ability to learn by smelling, hearing, seeing, touching, and, later on, observation and imitation. But Jason wasn't a baby. Tick poison had degraded his ability to process information, reduced his comprehension, and diminished his mnemonic understanding. He was slow, often exceedingly so, in connecting the dots. Jason couldn't catch a ball no matter how hard he tried, and it took him three times longer than any of his friends to add seven and eight. Human life is based on mental performance. Jason's mind had to be taught what it no longer knew how to do.

Yet teaching Jason quickly became a frustrating exercise—frustrating to him and frustrating to me. The problem was that he seemed unable to learn by instruction. When I tried to explain how to count or why clouds carry rain, his eyes glazed over, and he stopped listening, his mind incapable of connecting words to things. Jason knew a tree when he saw one, yet the word by itself meant nothing unless he stood in front of the actual tree. If Jason couldn't be taught in the conventional way, how did he learn? What was the pathway to his mind?

Jason knew many things: hundreds of animals and plants, his way around the mountain, and how Philyra expected him to behave. And while no one had told him the difference between an oak tree and a birch, he could tell one from the other and describe their different characteristics in the minutest detail. Having thus framed my question, the answer was simple enough: the mind learns either by being told what something is or by experiencing how something smells, feels, and looks. The first is instruction; the second is experience. Since instruction didn't work with Jason, experience would have to be his way of learning.

The idea of learning by experience ruffled my mind for hours on end before I hit on a way to make it work. Jason fancied adventure stories, tales of courageous men traveling across the seas in search of riches and unknown lands. So why not build a ship and sail to a distant place? Not a real journey, of course, but a make-believe game simulating the experience of a long and dangerous expedition. Why not develop a story-game about Jason steering a ship, commanding men, dealing with adversities, and making decisions to reach a distant goal?

Wouldn't such a game teach him how to think and act, how to deal and work with others, and how to choose between right and wrong? Frankly I wasn't sure. Life is not a game, and playing make-believe is not the same as actually feeling love or fearing death. But something had to be done, and since Jason was used to hearing a new story each night, I hoped that playing a game of making up a story wouldn't appear all that far-fetched to him.

NAUTIKA

Philyra had a difficult time with Jason while I was away visiting Kroronos. Disappointed that he couldn't accompany me, Jason threw a tantrum the minute I left, hurled the large stirrup jar against the wall, and refused to eat the barley gruel Philyra prepared in the morning. In his anger he ran up to the peak, oblivious of the mountain lions there; he returned only late at night and, refusing to come home, slept in Hagno's hut. Philyra was beside herself, sick of worrying for his safety and jealous because he had run to the wet nurse instead of to her.

Jason finally came home an hour before my return. Philyra was way too angry to deal with him and unsure how to cope with his unthinking defiance. I felt equally nonplussed, wondering whether Jason was volitionally disobedient because he didn't get his way or whether his mind had snapped when his wish was denied. He seemed more disturbed than upset, his squinty-tight eyes reflecting confusion and pain, albeit no remorse. Was he simply defiant or merely surprised by what he did? Had he discovered a side of himself he didn't know existed?

I took his hand and walked him across the goats' pasture,

suggesting we go up to the spring and dunk our heads in the ice-cold pool. When Jason laughed about cooling our heads, I knew he was anxious to talk.

"Jason, we didn't do a story last night. Should we do it now?"

"I guess so, but make it a voyage across the seas, sailing to places where no one has been before."

"Perhaps Pelops plowing the sea for sixty days before landing at Pisa?"

"No, not Pelops. I want to know about Phrixos, who sailed to Kolchis but never returned."

"But no one knows what happened to Phrixos. He ran away after quarreling with his father. Some say he drowned in rough weather. Others allege Amazons killed him. Then there's a Korinthian tale about Phrixos and his sister riding through the air on a golden-haired ram—a story no one but the stupid Hellenes can possibly believe to be true."

"Cheiron, if you don't know what happened, can't you pretend you do and tell me how you think Phrixos made it to Kolchis?"

Well, Jason gave me an opening, and I wasted little time insinuating my plan of engaging him in a story-game. I told him to forget about Phrixos and instead make believe that we were undertaking the voyage ourselves. Putting on my serious face, I suggested we pretend to build a ship, recruit a crew, and sail to Kolchis, with Jason acting as captain and the expedition's leader. His eyes lit up and he immediately played along, coming forth with a thousand suggestions about constructing the ship, hiring a crew, and how to pay for it all. He said we had to hire a shipwright to build the vessel. The shipwright had to be paid for his work and for the wood he needed.

"Cheiron, building a ship is expensive, which means

without money we won't be sailing anywhere soon. Who, I wonder, might finance a voyage to Kolchis?"

"A wealthy man thinking he can profit from the voyage."

"Well, the richest man in Thessaly is King Peleas of Iolkos."

"Yes, Jason, but Peleas's sole interest is power, not riches. All he wants is a large army and a hundred-horse cavalry."

"But Cheiron, Kolchis is rich in gold. Don't you think greedy Peleas will want that gold in order to hire more warriors and extend his rule?"

I was impressed: Jason clearly had a talent for playing the game, and he knew a lot more than I had ever surmised. Unaware that Peleas was his biological uncle, Jason correctly identified the king as the wealthiest man around. What's more he knew of the rumors about the gold of Kolchis and straightaway concluded that gold would be the king's motive for sponsoring the make-believe voyage. The rumors were that wild rivers carried tiny particles of gold from Kolchis's high mountains into the Euxine Sea. The local people placed sheepskins in the streams to trap the gold flecks, then hung the skins out to dry and shook them to recover the specks of gold. Jason's idea was to convince Peleas that if he sponsored the trip, the gold of Kolchis would be his. Jason also said Peleas's vile reputation didn't bother him as long as his wealth served the story-game's purpose.

Having decided on a sponsor, the next task was to recruit a shipbuilder of high repute, a master craftsman who could build a galley that was both sturdy and swift. Jason chose Argos, son of Arestor, whose very name stood for his skill in building superior ships. Argos would have to cut and hew the required timber and shape by axe pinewood for the hull and the oars, walnut for the ribs and struts, and oak for the keel, bow, and mast. He also had to saw the axe-felled pines into pliant planks and steam them over fire to fit the curvature of the strakes; wooden joints had to be daubed with sealing wax, and the hull had to be girded with a strong rope drawn taut on either side.

After we talked all day about building the ship—which plank to fit where and which joint to seal—a precise image of its form emerged. The finished ship was a beauty to behold, sleek and fast, her fifteen rowing benches and the helmsman's seat at the prow accommodating a crew of thirty-two. It was a vision of the mind, to be sure, but so intense were our imaginations that the make-believe vessel seemed as real as the fingers of my hand.

Philyra, waiting at the cave's outer door, encountered an utterly transformed Jason. Only yesterday the boy had been swearing and cussing and kicking furniture. Now he hugged his mother, told her how hungry he was, and babbled about Argos who had agreed to built him a ship. Philyra exhaled a sigh of relief while silently asking with a questioning glance what was going on and why Jason was talking about a ship. When Jason ran off to the kitchen to grab some food, I explained to Philyra that I was engaging him in a game of the mind, a story-game really, as a means to restore the mental functions the ticks had destroyed.

Philyra shook her head in disbelief. Pretend to sail a ship to the Euxine Sea? How stupid was that? What Jason needed was good food and regular exercise, not an impossible story that bore no relation to reality. Pretending to build a ship on top of a mountain was nonsense, an exercise in delusion, and no way to bring back the boy's mental faculties.

While Philyra didn't like playing with Jason's mind, she had to admit that the boy was excited about the story-game idea and most eager to participate. Always practical and willing to try any cure, Philyra at last relented, suggesting we both pursue our separate therapies: she would feed Jason and supervise his daily training while I would try to rebuild his mind by pretending to sail to Kolchis. And that's what we did over the next two years. From the start Jason embraced the game with unbridled zest, his mind immediately jumping ahead to the delicate task of assembling a suitable crew. But the story-game had to be developed at a lifelike pace in order for the story to feel real. Not everything could happen right away; rather events had to unfold step by step, as if the story were proceeding in real time. Though eager to hurry on, Jason accepted my advice and agreed to postpone the recruiting process until the next day.

Sailing across the Euxine Sea obviously required superior mates—oarsmen who were exceptionally strong and predisposed to work as a team. Rowing requires muscular strength: the stronger the rowers, the faster the ship cuts through the waves, provided everyone rows as one. Jason wasn't sure what I meant by the need for cooperation among the crew. Wasn't the voyage a unique adventure, and wouldn't each member of the crew want to succeed? Well, yes, but everyone doing his best didn't necessarily mean everyone was going to do what was best for the ship. Each of the thirty-two men was likely to disagree on which course to take, when to raise sail, where to make landfall, and how to deal with natives on foreign shores.

Jason's effectiveness as captain of the ship would also depend on the crew's respect for him and for each other. Teamwork requires individualist subordination, with each member willing to put the team ahead of himself—something not everyone would be willing to do. Ideally the crew would be a band of brothers, men supporting each other like siblings born to the same mother. And though there was no chance of finding thirty-two brothers or even thirty-two cousins, we thought we could find thirty-two men who hailed from the same tribe and spoke the same language, namely Minyans who lived in the region stretching from Boiotia in the south to Thessaly in the north. Jason still wasn't convinced about the compatibility thing, but he was happy that most of the Argonauts would speak his Aeolian dialect.

Our most important task was hiring an experienced helmsman, one able to steer the ship by the stars and sense the coming of a swell across the sea. A certain Tiphys, a Minyan living in Siphae on the Korinthian Gulf, was reputed to be the best, and he was our immediate choice. Tiphys, of course, required capable assistants—men who could predict the weather, spot currents and eddies, and safely anchor the ship at night. After much deliberation we selected Mopsos from Titaressa and Idmon from sea-girded Argolida. We also agreed to invite sweet-tempered Orpheus to join the crew, knowing that his voice and lyre would steady the rhythm of the oarsmen's strokes. We assembled the first three members of the ship's crew by the end of the day. Jason couldn't wait to tell Philyra who would be joining his team.

Eating spit-roasted chicken at supper, Philyra was deeply happy to have the old Jason back, older in years and acting the way he had before the ticks had invaded his body. Visibly pumped up and stuttering a lot, Jason was all business, telling Philyra that Argos, the famous shipwright, was busy building the ship, and that Tiphys, Mopsos, and Idmon had signed on. Philyra, unsure how to react to Jason's fantasy tale, quietly asked for the ship's name. Well, it didn't have one, not yet, and Jason, unable to invent a name on the spot, suddenly seemed overcome by his old feelings of incompetence. For the ship to be real, it had to have a name, or the whole notion of sailing to

Kolchis was but a dream. Sensing that Jason's self-confidence was at stake, Philyra's quick wit saved the day: Didn't Argos build the ship? And wasn't it true that without Argos there would be no ship? And didn't this mean the ship should be named after its builder, and wouldn't Argo be a good name? One that honored the ship's builder and also referred to her speed.

The boy hesitated, waiting for my reaction. When I nodded my head in assent he jumped up and planted a mushy kiss on Philyra's right cheek.

Jason and I spent the next several months assembling the rest of the crew and launching the ship. Word that Tiphys and Mopsos had joined the expedition traveled fast and far, sparking interest throughout the Hellenic lands. Rather than us looking for Argonauts, we were swamped by volunteers eager to sign up for the voyage. The first and most avid to join was Herakles, one of Zeus's many sons. Herakles had no interest in Kolchis or gold; his sole aim was to accumulate glory, to engage in battle and kill the largest number of foes. While he was undoubtedly brave and tremendously strong, his horrific temper and lack of impulse control had led to mayhem and death time and again. So fearsome was Herakles's reputation that no one openly questioned his physical strength or the merit of his argument, lest the great man felt compelled to add another victim to his already long list. Herakles was not an innately bad guy, but his lone-wolf mentality was like a dormant volcano—a mere threat when asleep, but deadly when aflame. Yet rejecting him was well nigh impossible. No one, least of all King Peleas, who financed the expedition, would agree to shut out the greatest warrior of our time. So, despite our misgivings, we welcomed Herakles and thanked him for bringing along young Hylas, his protégé and traveling muse.

With Herakles a member of the crew, assembling a reasonably harmonious team acquired new urgency. Jason suggested we look for pairs of brothers, each brother being the natural ally of the other. In time we identified five effectively complementary pairs—Kastor and Polydeukes, Eryton and Echion, Kalais and Zetes, Areius and Talaos, and Peleus and Telamon—and invited them to join the team. Jason, proud of his recruitment proposal, was right in believing that hiring ten brothers would go a long way toward realizing the band-of-brothers idea. He was beginning to think logically—an early indication that the story-game project could have the desired educational effect.

The ten brothers Jason recruited were battle-hardened and exceedingly strong, but the ship remained woefully short of men experienced in seamanship and various specialized skills. Taking my advice to heart, Jason doubled his effort. He searched for names and did necessary background checks, and ultimately chose Nauplios and Idmon for navigation, Ankaeos and gray-haired Erginos as substitute helmsmen, Aethalides to keep the log, Argos to maintain the ship in good repair, and Eribotes to do the same for the members of the crew. After manning these positions, we had nine more places to fill.

An obvious additional choice was Meleagros, who had killed the Kalydonian boar; another was Euphemos, a swift runner who could cross over water. A third was Periklymenos, the super-strong son of Neleus. Others who enlisted in quick order were Polyphemos from Larissa, Oileus from Lokris, Iphitos of Phokis, Leodokos from Argos, and Idas who was born in distant Messenia. Last but not least—and to everyone's surprise—King Peleas's son, Akostos, volunteered. Although he was young and inexperienced, we didn't dare to reject him. We assigned him the left seat on the rear-most rowing bench.

When Nessos stopped by the cave the following night, Jason told him all about Argo and her crew. Without raising an eyebrow or otherwise acting incredulous, Nessos listened to Jason's account, frequently asking detailed questions. Jason quickly invented answers on the spot. But when he reported Herakles was joining the crew, Nessos became deeply upset, jumped from his chair, and paced the length of the dining alcove, asserting that Herakles was a treacherous brute who killed for fun—or what the Hellenes called glory—and that letting him join the crew was a colossal mistake.

With my ears tuned to Jason's narration, I didn't immediately realize that Nessos's tirade was lurching out of control. Surely he understood that Jason's account was not about anything real because, after all, there was no crew, no ship, and no voyage. The fact that Herakles was a real person rather than merely a myth seemed to have fooled Nessos into believing that what Jason told him was real too. Nessos hated Herakles with such passion that he confused fiction with reality; his emotions negated his reason even though he must have been fully aware that Herakles couldn't possibly be anywhere near the fantasy ship Jason was talking about.

After allowing Nessos to rant for several embarrassing minutes, Jason earnestly explained that Herakles was only one of thirty-two shipmates and that sailing the feared Euxine Sea would surely discourage anyone from acting up. Nessos took a deep breath and slowly regained his composure.

With the crew fully assembled and chafing at the bit, the time had come to launch the ship. Argos had the men dig a trench from the ship's prow to the edge of the water. Then he had them place rollers on the bottom of the trench and attach hawsers to the sides of the ship. Argos signaled to the men to haul away with all their strength, and they slowly pulled sleek Argo inch by inch into Pagasae Bay. As the ship came to rest in the water, the men fit oars to locks and set the mast with forestays drawn taut on either side. The oarsmen drew lots for their places on the fifteen benches, with each bench accommodating two men, one at starboard and the other at port.

Rocking gently in the evening breeze, Jason was anxious to cast off before the sun would hide behind the Pindos Mountains. But the Hellenic crew loudly demurred, insisting on offering an appropriate sacrifice to one of their confounded gods. Who, I asked myself, had told Jason about the Hellenes' sick practice of killing animals to please Zeus and his Olympian family? Jason's source was Pholos, of course, the good-for-nothing Hellenophile who lived on the northern side of the mountain and believed that unless the Hellenic gods smelled the sweet odor of an animal's entrails, punishment would rain on mortal men.

Jason claimed he didn't believe any of Pholos's religious babble but considered it unwise to risk the wrath of a god without knowing for sure that he didn't exist. In any case, he brusquely demanded to perform an actual sacrifice instead of merely talking about it.

"Jason, no! Remember we are playing a story-game, pretending to sail to Kolchis without actually going there. We talk as if we are building a ship, but there is no real ship. No part of our story is real, least of all the pointless sacrifice of an animal, which is something we would never do—something our people haven't done for centuries."

"Yes, Cheiron, I know. Neither the ship nor the crew is really real, but don't you want me to experience the story as if it were true? Since it is difficult to believe that what we pretend is real, an actual sacrifice would bridge the gap between fiction and reality and make at least one part of the story physically true. Yesterday you brought home ten new sheep. Why can't we sacrifice one of them? If we do, our make-believe game will be a lot more believable."

"No, it will not. Killing a sheep would be real, you got that right, but killing a sheep wouldn't make the Argo story any more real than it is. There is no relationship between what we do up here on the mountain and the story we say is happening on Pagasae Bay. And with barely enough food for the winter, it makes no earthly sense to waste a precious animal for the sole purpose of establishing a false correspondence between fiction and fact."

My harshly worded response spread perplexity over Jason's young face. He jumped from his chair and ran off into the woods, leaving me in fear that the whole project had come to an end. Philyra witnessed the whole conversation and told me, in no uncertain terms, that if I wanted Jason to sail a ship to Kolchis, I couldn't treat him like a boy but had to deal with him as if he were a grown-up man fully capable of commanding a ship. For the make-believe game to work, Jason had to buy in to the story, and for the ship to depart in the morning, I had to bring Jason back into the game.

The next morning was chilly and overcast, with wind gusts forming pesky white crowns on the bay's rolling waves. The Argonauts stood shivering on the beach while Argos and his helpers hauled the ship close to shore for the men to stow arms and equipment and take their allotted seats on the rowing benches. All thirty-two members of the crew were in excellent spirits, happy that the long-awaited voyage was about to begin, and doubly happy that congenial Jason, rather than volatile Herakles, would lead the expedition.

Choosing Jason over Herakles had engendered an awkward moment or two. All along the plan had been for Jason to be Argo's captain in order for him to acquire real-life experience, albeit in simulated form. Yet Herakles was senior to Jason in every respect. He was immensely strong, had an excellent military record, and was renowned throughout the Hellenic world. He was rated best by the men, making the ship's captaincy his well-deserved due. Yet his erratic character troubled many, and some mistrusted his motives out of hand.

Herakles, rarely one to deceive himself, sensed the crew's ambivalence and declined to seek the captainship, proposing instead that Jason be the expedition's leader. Jason thanked his Hellenic mates for their confidence, and, mindful of their age-old rituals, poured wine into the gray sea in honor of their supposedly deathless gods. Then Jason raised his sword and cut the anchor rope with one mighty blow. Argo was on its way.

Tiphys manned the sideways-steering oar, Nauplios set the ship's course straight south to exit Pagasae Bay at Cape Aianteion, and the men lowered their oars, striking the rolling sea to the beat of Orpheus's lyre. But, as increasingly heavy gusts whipped the water, Argo's progress became maddeningly erratic, giving the oarsmen an early taste of the pain of rowing under stress. When the wind rose to gale-like strength, the crew was forced to match the storm's growing power lest Tiphys lose control of the ship. With water-laced gusts lashing the rowers' faces and setting their muscles on fire, all count of time was lost in the fight to stay afloat. The ship had to face each wave head on or be flooded and sink. Desperately trying to survive, the Argonauts merged with their oars, making the implements virtual extensions of themselves. This was not what the men had expected. They had signed up for a cruise to an unexplored corner of the world, but now, barely an hour into the voyage, they had to exert body and soul to keep their lives.

Jason was at his wits' desperate end, terrified by the gale-whipped sea and deathly afraid of drowning. He had been prepared for endless hours of rowing, aware that it would be hard work, but the ferocity of the storm and the threat of drowning while barely out of port numbed his mind with fear. He had thought of the voyage as play and now watched in horror as it turned into terror, death looming with each crashing wave. Rowing no longer was a means to an end but an end in itself. It was row or die, their only choice to keep pulling their oars through the surging sea.

Yet the oarsmen's rhythmic strokes also worked to push back their own fears and channeled their individual efforts into a single force. Coming at the beginning of the voyage, the storm molded the Argonauts into a true team, creating one body out of thirty-two. The crew's performance would have been perfect, or almost so, if it hadn't been for Herakles's huge size and heavy weight. He rowed harder than anyone onboard, but his powerful strokes tended to pull Argo toward port at the same time that his weight caused the ship to tilt left. Tiphys did his best to meet each incoming wave head on, but due to the ship's leftward list the hull was repeatedly flooded with the bay's salt-sodden water. Although Herakles, more than any other, saved Argo from sinking during the storm, his huge bulk almost caused the ship to capsize and sink.

Luckily the storm abated as suddenly as it had come, the sun breaking through the scattering clouds and the wind changing from turbulent chaos to a faint southeasterly breeze, albeit too weak to propel the ship by itself. Realizing the crew needed time to recover, Jason decided to hoist the square sail and allow the men to pull up their oars and stretch out on the narrow deck. Tiphys alone remained at his post, steering the slowly drifting ship southward to Cape Aianteion, where Pagasae Bay merges into the Aegean Sea.

At supper that night, when Jason recounted Argo's first day of sailing, Nessos questioned the ship's rapid progress across Pagasae Bay and past Cape Aianteion, saying no rowing crew, however strong, could row so far in a single day. Jason heatedly insisted on his account, asserting that Argo's rapid passage was due to the violent storm's blowing it across the bay in little more than an hour. Jason further asserted, while nibbling on a chunk of cheese, that the ship had a strong breeze at its back and was rushing past the Tisaean headland and Pelion's rocky southern coast toward seagirt Skiathos Isle. Then, as Argo rounded Cape Sepias, the wind miraculously shifted from east to north and filled her sail again, driving the ship northward along the wild Magnesian coast.

Jason explained that the bone-tired crew wanted to call it a day, but as Argo's captain he was unwilling to forego the stiff breeze, and kept the sail unfurled until the wind faded late at night. Only then, with the sea completely becalmed, did the mates brail the sail to the yard and, under a starless sky, row Argo to Aphetae beach, near Peiresiae town.

With the ship safely beached, Philyra clapped her hands in joy, telling Jason what a wonderful story he had told and that it was time for him to go to bed. Nessos, however, was less impressed, and loudly complained that Jason's ship was traveling impossibly fast, killing the story's verisimilitude. Wasn't the purpose of the story-game to teach Jason about life as it really was? And shouldn't he learn things that are true, rather than be made to believe that Argo sails four times faster than a real ship?

Nessos, easily hot under the collar and ever the rationalist, accused me of misleading rather than educating the boy, making him a dreamer instead of a doer. And not just a dreamer but a superstitious dreamer—one who poured good wine into the sea believing some imaginary god would reciprocate in a favorable way. Why, Nessos demanded to know, was Jason taught religion when everyone knew that the Hellenic gods were fairytale blowhards, creatures of a primitive imagination, born out of ignorance? Science had cured Jason's disorder, not prayers and sacrifices. His libation was a waste of perfectly good wine.

Of course he was right. No ship could sail the distance Jason claimed Argo had covered on her first day at sea. And Nessos was right about the Hellenic gods too. Religion is the opposite of knowledge—faith devoid of material evidence. But whether to familiarize Jason with the basic tenets of the Hellenic religion was a different matter. As Philyra kept saying, Jason would be living his life as a Hellene among Hellenes and would be obliged to conform to Hellenic customs and rituals whether he believed in their gods or not. If a Hellene refuses to sacrifice to the gods, he is considered a danger not only to himself but to his whole community. Since Jason was about to steer Argo into harm's way, it was essential that he observed the Hellenic religion, or run the risk of losing his crew's trust. For Jason to be an effective leader, his crew had to believe that their gods looked on the voyage with beneficence.

"Nessos, don't you see? Jason has no choice but to go through the motions of observing Hellenic religious practice. His Minyan crew fully expects their leader to honor and respect their gods. It doesn't matter what Jason believes. What matters is that the crew trusts him. Face it—religion does have its uses. Man's confidence invariably grows when he believes that the gods are on his side."

"But Cheiron, what you say is dishonest and an insult to reason. Religion, like anything else, is either true or false, and if it's false it can't be good. To claim that whatever is useful is good makes a mockery of the concept of good. A lie is a lie regardless of what purpose it serves."

"Nessos, calm down. We are not talking about the good, whatever that is. We are dealing with Jason, who has to convince his crew to row a leaky ship to the end of the world. Since it is impossible either to prove or disprove the gods' existence, talking about them is really meaningless. I will not teach Jason any religion, but, by the same token, I will not dispute whatever he may hear from Pholos or some other faith-inclined, trusting soul. It's up to Jason to decide what, if anything, he wants to believe. But you are right about the distance covered by the ship on the first day. Going forward, Jason's narrative has to stay within the bounds of what is physically possible and avoid supernatural fantasies."

I was busy at the school the next day and also the day after, returning home long after Jason had gone to bed. But the boy was eager to continue the Argo adventure, and on the third night persuaded Philyra to let him wait up for me. We began discussing Nessos's objections and why Jason refused to revise the ship's first day at sea. Declaring that no one, not even the gods, had the power to change the past, he agreed the first day was a sequence of improbable events unlikely to occur in reality. For the story to be real, all of it had to be real, and Jason promised there would be no further recourse to miracles and such. Rather, as if to demonstrate his newfound sense of reality, he expressed genuine concern about his men's physical condition after their long and exhausting first day. Since we hadn't worked on the story-game for two days, he had given his men time off to recuperate on Aphetae beach. But when the wind picked up at sunrise, blowing northeast in line with Nauplios's charted course, Jason roused the mates and resumed the voyage in haste.

Jason was thrilled that the crew, who were restless after sitting on the beach for two long, boring days, eagerly clambered onboard while the sun had yet to stretch her rose-colored fingers across the virgin sky. The men rowed the ship out into open water and, still in sight of the shore, unfurled the square sail to catch the strong southern breeze. Argo's sleek prow cut through the water with ease, gracing the wine-colored sea with a beautiful, foam-crested wake. The ship, hugging the Thessalian coast, plowed northward, and in quick order passed the settlements of Meliboea, Omolion, and Eurymenae before reaching the mouth of the Amyrus River, whose vigorous outflow caused the ship to veer away from land.

Although night was falling, Tiphys took advantage of both current and wind and steered the ship due east, soon coming in sight of Cape Canastra on Pallene's southern tip, the westernmost spur of the Chalkidiki Peninsula. With the wind at their back, Jason decided to sail on through the night until the crew looked in awe at Athos's towering mountains in the early morning light. Then the wind faded, and an eerie calm settled over the Aegean Sea. The ship sat still. What was to be done? Await a breeze on the open sea, beach the ship on the steep coast of Athos, or row south to fair Lemnos?

Waiting for a breeze in the middle of the Aegean was an uncertain bet. The calm wouldn't last forever, and a new wind could blow in any direction and leave the ship worse off rather than better. Scanning the dangerously craggy shoreline of the Athos peninsula, neither Tiphys nor Nauplios were able to spot a place even remotely suitable for anchoring the ship. Clearly, landing on Athos was out. Equally problematic was rowing the ship all the way to Lemnos, because it would conscript the crew to hard labor for the rest of the day—not what anyone wanted to do. Yet Jason asked the Argonauts to do just that, choosing what he thought was the least risky course of action and exactly what an experienced mariner would have done.

So, on the sixth day of the voyage, the men brailed the sail and, sighing in dread, took their seats on the rowing benches. Herakles and Ankaeos claimed the middle row. Placing their oars into the tholes and taking deep breaths, the Argonauts resigned themselves to rowing all day.

Orpheus strung his lyre and sang of deathless Artemis, the protectress of sailors and ships. The rowers' motion flowed with the music, their blades attacking the sea in sync and creating a barely visible wake behind the slow-moving ship. The forward swing and backward pull of the rowing stroke became an endless chain of pain, gradually inching the ship toward Lemnos thirty miles south. With the sea deadly calm and the sun blazing hot, the only sounds were Orpheus's sweet song, the oarsmen's labored breath, and the sea's lazy lapping against the ship's hull. Herakles rowed hardest of all, but, as before, his disproportionate weight caused Argo to list to port. The men worked extremely hard, and by early afternoon heat and exhaustion had transformed the crew into a mindless machine gulping down gallons of the water they had bottled at the spring of Aphetae.

Yet rowing Argo was not like plowing a field, felling a tree, or hunting for game. The Argonauts had signed up for the voyage knowing full well that on windless days their muscle power would be the ship's sole means of locomotion, making rowing the essence of the voyage—hard work, yes, but also play, a game of pleasure for the glory it entailed. And so, after hours of working and playing by the sweat of their brows, the Argonauts came within sight of the island of Lemnos, where crowds of people could be seen milling about on the beach. However, barely an hour later, when the ship finally came to rest on the beach, there was no one to greet the exhausted crew.

What should the Argonauts have done? Spend the night on the beach, or try to find a friendlier place? The consensus was to stay put if only because the men, their hands covered with blisters, were too tired to row another mile. At sea for a day, a night, and a second day, the crew had reached its physical limit. Since Jason had promised to shun improbable scenarios, the crew didn't move on because they couldn't. Yet the shipmates were uneasy, and rightly so, not knowing whether the islanders were friendly or hostile, either case being equally likely. Jason, for one, didn't like the fifty-fifty odds and quietly ordered well-spoken Aethalides to reconnoiter the island, locate the local king, and formally ask permission for the Argonauts to spend the night at the beach. Aethalides was taken aback by Jason's request but nonetheless accepted the hazardous mission.

Fear walked with Aethalides as he left the ship. Who were these islanders, and what kind of king did they have? Were they Hellenes or barbarians? Did they honor guest friendship or rob and kill whoever washed up on their shores? It was only too obvious why Jason sent him to scout the island alone, without any companions or guards: if the islanders gave Aethalides a friendly reception, all would be fine, but if their intentions were hostile, only one of the thirty-two-strong crew would be lost.

So Aethalides was afraid, feeling like a tethered goat surrounded by growling dogs, with shadows hovering all around. Cautiously treading his way, he looked for a path to the town where the islanders lived, but the night's dark blanket was close to impenetrable, his eyes unable to see more than a foot ahead. He knew not where he was and felt utterly lost.

Suddenly three heavily armed soldiers blocked his way, asking his name and intent.

"I am Aethalides, herald of the Argonauts. Please take me to your king."

"Our sovereign is Queen Hypsipyle. What is the purpose of your request?"

"We seek permission to spend the night on your beach."

"Go back to your ship. You will be told of the queen's decision."

On his return to the ship, Aethalides gave Jason a precise report of his encounter with the island guards. Reluctantly, and feeling somewhat embarrassed, Aethalides told Jason the soldiers were women, not men; that Lemnos was ruled by a queen, not a king; and that the queen would render her decision at her convenience. Jason shook his head, not knowing what to make of it all, but thought it best to wait for the queen's reply.

Waiting, however, is easier said than done, and Jason certainly had no experience with waiting to hear from a mysterious queen. When no islander showed up within an hour or so, Jason panicked and woke me in the middle of night, saying he didn't know how to continue the story-game because he didn't know what was going to happen next. Would the Lemnian queen welcome him or launch an attack?

Dragging me from sleep in the middle of night was neither smart nor considerate. It was Jason, not I, who worried about the island queen. I was safe in my cave and fast asleep, not on some foreign beach feeling afraid of a queen. I told Jason waiting was his only choice, pulled a fleece over my head, and went back to sleep.

As it turned out, my irritated response was good advice, for within the very next hour an emissary appeared at the beach, asking Jason to come to the palace and meet the queen. Anxious to present himself as a peaceful explorer instead of a seafaring raider, Jason put on his embroidered cloak, tied on his finely wrought sandals, and wisely left behind his arms. As he walked through the town on his way to the palace, throngs of women gawked at his wardrobe, but none said a word. As he approached the palace gate, the double doors were opened; two female guards checked him for weapons, and a third escorted him to the megaron.

There Jason came face to face with the queen. He was stunned. Hypsipyle was beautiful—the most beautiful woman he had ever seen. Her blue eyes glittered like diamonds at dusk; blonde locks framed her elegantly narrow face, and the line of her figure was nature as art. Transfixed by her appearance, Jason was speechless, as was the queen, who saw him not as the felonious invader he was but as the consort her heart had long desired. Unable to hide her welling emotions, a roseate blush spread across her lovely face as she struggled to lower her eyes.

Jason was first to recover his wits and petitioned the queen to allow his crew to camp at the beach. Hypsipyle immediately granted permission and invited Jason and his men to come into town and meet her people. Jason gladly accepted, though his puzzled expression betrayed his concern over the apparent absence of men. Where were they? Would they attack the ship while the queen pretended to receive Jason as a friend? Had he fallen into a deadly trap?

Sensing his concern, Hypsipyle explained that only women lived on Lemnos. There were no men. In years past the men of Lemnos had raided the coast of Thraki, bringing home bounty and female slaves. In time some of the men married their slaves, but what began as an aberration became an obsession; every man on the island cast aside his legitimate wife and married a Thrakian whore. The men's behavior violated ancestral law, and the women of Lemnos resolved to right the wrong. Hellenic to the core, and proud descendants of gods and heroes, no man would shove them aside, least of all their hornswoggling former mates.

So the women confronted the men with a choice: either send away their slaves and offspring, or leave the island for good. Well, the men chose to leave, and for the past ten years the island had been blessed with prosperity and peace—though not, as Hypsipyle was quick to admit, with true happiness for all. For obvious reasons no children had been born in a long while, and life without men was less than fulfilling. Such being the case, the queen invited the Argonauts to visit the town, meet the women, and remain as long as they wished.

When Jason returned to the ship and reported the queen's invitation, the mates yelled "yippee!" and "doo-da-la-doo!"

They were ready to rush into town, meet up with the women, play games, and have fun. Herakles alone scoffed at the men's display of immaturity, rejected the invitation, and stayed on the beach to guard the ship. Jason, smitten by Hypsipyle's charm, quickly guided his men to the main town, and soon the whole island was busy dancing, drinking, and diddling all through the day and into the next. Musical competitions and athletic contests were held, with gray-haired Erginos winning the footrace and receiving the victor's wreath from the queen.

The men drank, ate, and paired up with the women while Hypsipyle artfully tried to seduce Jason in her chambers, her wiles aimed at keeping him on Lemnos forever. Without a royal husband the Lemnian dynasty would end with her; without mates the island's population would die out in not many years. Hypsipyle knew in her heart that without men her people were doomed. It made no sense for her to hold back. She had to make Jason an offer he couldn't refuse.

Locking eyes with her handsome guest, Queen Hypsipyle boldly suggested Jason and she should marry, and for him to assume the Lemnian throne. Hypsipyle's simple logic was to offer Jason all she had, including herself, in order to get what she and her people had to have. Surely no sane man in the whole wide world would reject both her kingdom and her. Yet Jason reacted in unexpected fashion. He had come to the palace asking for camping rights on the beach and found the queen offering him not only free camping but also herself and all of Lemnos too. So he hesitated, undefined questions troubling his mind, including his oath to complete the Kolchian quest. Hypsipyle, however, was determined to get her way, and in a fiery display of passion dissuaded Jason from leaving her bed.

This could have been the end of the story-game, with Jason forgetting about Kolchis and staying on Lemnos forever. But it so happened that Herakles chose this very moment to summon the Argonauts to a special meeting at the ship. Herakles was furious, scolding the men for abandoning their sworn quest to take the gold of Kolchis. The purpose of their voyage was glory, not to copulate and repopulate the Lemnian isle. Glory was achieving the near impossible, excelling and being victorious, not snuggling in bed, frolicking with hordes of sex-starved spinsters. If Jason, the captain of the ship, preferred Hypsipyle to immortal fame, he should stay and cuddle, but the rest of the crew, Hellenic warriors all descended from gods and heroes, were obligated by blood and oath to uphold their national tradition.

The men listened to Herakles's repute in silence, aware that the insult thrown at Jason was equally aimed at them. It was, of course, easy for Herakles to deride female pleasures when sweet, little Hylas, his young protégé, did exactly the same for him. Herakles was a hypocrite, and the men resented him for that, but he also happened to be right about glory and ethos, and the men resented him for that too.

And yet the men remained of two minds, the certainty of leisure and love competing with the fickle prospect of glory and gold. What the men most desired would be theirs if they made Lemnos their home. Mopsos, however, wasn't so sure, wondering whether one or two days of pleasure would guarantee happiness to the end of one's days. In fact, Mopsos declared, the women's story didn't make a whole lot of sense: no honorable man would marry his slave. It seemed more likely that the men had been kicked out by their wives and were forced to move on. Whatever the case, something seemed fishy about

Hypsipyle's tale, and basing a life decision on two happy-go-lucky days seemed overly rash.

What really happened on Lemnos? Was it the fault of the men or the women? If the Lemnian women couldn't please their own men, how would they treat thirty-two Hellenes? None of the Argonauts had a convincing answer. Doubt crept into their hearts, and the more they thought the more confused they became, unable to compare one unknown to another. Would living on Lemnos bring happiness? What was happiness anyhow? Staying on Lemnos would mean peace and prosperity while sailing to Kolchis meant danger, risk, and possibly death! But was Lemnos really without risk? Did they really know why there wasn't a single man on the island, not even a toddler or a young boy?

Herakles, sensing the debate was swinging his way, pointed out that the Argonauts knew only what the women had told them—there was no proof of anything—and slyly suggested the women may have killed the men.

Peleus angrily objected, calling it a malicious trick to spread fear among the men. Wasn't it true that Hypsipyle had offered to make Jason king, and wouldn't this guarantee their safety? Herakles merely shook his head, calling Peleus blindly naïve. Since there were hundreds of women but only thirty-two of them, the Argonauts would be badly outnumbered and liable to share the same fate as the mysteriously absent Lemnian men. Herakles's arguments, whatever their merit, sobered the men's thoughts: remaining on the island no longer seemed without risk. Ever so subtly the crew's sentiment began to shift.

Seizing the moment Herakles recalled with pride the countless labors he had endured, how he had never forsaken a task and always completed what he set out to do. There is no virtue in pleasure; excellence is the measure of man; what matters is glory and fame. To remain on Lemnos would be like staying in bed—something a woman or an old person might do—while rowing sleek Argo to Kolchis was a glorious deed that would be remembered till the end of time. Having thus spoken Herakles boarded the ship, and every member of the crew followed his lead. The Lemnian women, stunned by the debate's sudden turn, cried and lamented their fate, but the Argonauts were on their way.

"Jason, why were you silent at Herakles's meeting?"

"I was of two minds. If I stayed on Lemnos, I would have Hypsipyle and become king. If I sailed to Kolchis, I might become wealthy and still gain a wife."

"That's how you saw your choice?"

"Well, yes and no! My real choice was between a bird in hand and two in the bush, between virtual certainty and a great deal of risk. Most times certainty is best, but comparing Lemnos to Kolchis was not as simple as that."

"And why was that?"

"Lemnos had its own uncertainties, mainly the absence of men. Staying there would have meant comfort and leisure, but the lure of Kolchian gold easily compensated for the greater risk."

"So you prefer gold to happiness?"

"Frankly I don't know, but I didn't dare to challenge Herakles in open debate. The guy has killed good men for less than that."

Jason's account troubled me deeply. Only a week ago he had pledged to continue the story-game in a generally credible manner, yet straightaway the boy invented an island peopled solely by single women. And after spending one night with the island's queen, she offered to make him king, presumably in order to keep doing what they did. No doubt lusty desire and wishful thinking had invaded Jason's mind, or whatever he thought was involved in sharing a woman's bed. Philyra and Nessos insisted that Jason was too young to know about sex, but the boy must have heard something about something, or he wouldn't have landed the ship on an amatory paradise.

Since merely hearing about sex doesn't come close to experiencing the actual act, Jason's rejection of Hypsipyle's offer was necessarily based on incomplete and possibly wrong information. If thirteen-year-old Jason had known then what he came to know later, his likely choice would have been to marry the queen. Surely the whole crew, with the exception of Herakles, preferred comfort and ease to rowing a leaky ship across the treacherous Euxine Sea! But Jason didn't know any better, and the story-game resumed its predestined course.

Upon leaving Lemnos Jason's immediate goal was to reach the southern entrance of the Hellespont, the narrow strait that separates Europe from Asiatic Anatolia. The most direct route is to sail east to Tenedos Island and then run north along the Anatolian coast. Another way is to sail northeast, pass Imbros Island at portside and then steer north. The third route is to head north to Samothraki Island and then turn east, passing Imbros at starboard before reaching Cape Mastusia, the southern tip of the Chersonisos Peninsula that forms the European side of the Hellespont.

When Jason asked my advice, I was happy to counsel him. The main consideration in setting Argo's course was the dynamics of the Euxine Sea, a huge inland basin that collects the waters of numerous rivers. The river waters' only way out of the basin is the two-pronged channel formed by the Bosporos and the Hellespont. Since the two straits are quite narrow, the outflowing water accelerates sharply when passing through, thus creating powerful currents all the way south to Tenedos Island. And the strength of the current makes it close to impossible to row a galley up the channel without the help of a stiff southern breeze.

If the downward current of the Hellespont wasn't trouble enough, Troy's blockade of the shipping lane posed an even greater threat. Four years ago the Hellenic army finally invaded the plain of Troy, but in Jason's day the Trojan kings controlled the entrance to the Hellespont, monopolizing the slave trade as well as the import of Euxine metals and grain. In the context of the story-game, the Trojan navy surely would do all it could to prevent Argo from entering the Hellespont channel.

"Jason, which course will you set to the Hellespont?"

"Cheiron, none of the routes are perfect. All have flaws. The Tenedos course is most direct but goes against the Hellespont current, and we run the risk of being spotted by the Trojans there. The Imbros alternative is less affected by the current, but the Trojan risk is much the same. We have the best chance of escaping Troy's watchful eyes with the Samothraki route, but it's forty miles longer, which would mean a long extra day of rowing."

"So what's your decision?"

"I don't know. The crew won't row the additional forty miles, and neither Tiphys nor Nauplios knows how to round Cape Mastusia. I need time to think."

"But you have all the facts. Postponing the decision solves nothing. The time to act is now!"

Alas my advice went unheeded. Jason, unsure of the crew's allegiance, solicited everyone's view, hoping to reach a consensus. Herakles, however, wasn't interested in what others had to say, and loudly proclaimed that only cowards feared the Trojans and if others wanted to row an additional forty miles they would have to do so without him. Periklymenos claimed the most direct route was always the best and that Nauplios, the ship's official navigator, should make the decision. Yet Nauplios demurred, saying the tricky part was to catch a favorable breeze up the Hellespont, which prompted Zetes to warn that the south wind was notoriously fickle, active one day but absent the next.

Responding to Zetes's warning, Peleus argued that since they had to wait for the right wind in any case, the most sensible strategy was to sail from Samothraki to the western side of the Chersonisos and hide there from Trojan eyes until a southern breeze arose. Herakles disagreed, claiming no wind was needed to get through the strait—muscle power was enough, and he had plenty of that. Yet the more he talked, the less sense he made, and when none of the shipmates dared to contradict the great man, Tiphys boldly reset the steering blade, shifting the ship's prow to north.

With Samothraki set as their next objective, the crew rowed with renewed determination across a motionless sea, all humid and hot, not a whisper of breeze. The shipmates were obliged to row throughout the day, their hands covered with blisters, while Orpheus's sweet song wove their oar strokes into a rhythmic beat. At last, as the sun settled into the sea and darkness began to fall, Samothraki's volcano-shaped mountain came into view. Jason decided to beach the ship for the night and, on Mopsos's advice, asked an island priest to sacrifice a goat to the local Kabeiri gods. The men were bone-tired and quickly sank into sleep, grateful that a goat's life had bought them a restful night.

Yet when seven hours of night gave way to a new day, the Bay of Melas was as pitilessly hot as the previous day, humid and without any wind. The men put blistery hands to bloody oars and commenced rowing under the burning sun. But doubt filled their hearts—doubt about the purpose of it all, and serious doubt about leaving Lemnos against their baser desires. Had they remained on the blessed isle, they would have been eating lunch and playing nookie instead of suffering on the murderous open sea. Herakles had talked of fame and glory but surely there was no virtue in rowing for hours on end, their muscles twisted in painful cramps. Yet turning back was not an option, the men knew that too, so they rowed on throughout the day until they made landfall behind Cape Mastusia as the sun made way for the night.

Moored in darkness on the lee side of the Chersonisos Peninsula, the ship was hidden from hostile Trojans eyes, allowing the crew to rest their tired bodies while waiting for a favorable wind. Kalais was first to notice a tiny riffle on the water's surface, followed by a second and a third, each barely perceivable as the sea stirred ever so slightly. Holding a wetted finger aloft, Kalais felt air faintly flowing from the south. He woke Jason, who in turn immediately roused the men, urging them to row the ship around the cape and unfurl the sail at the entrance of the Hellespont Strait. With the breeze gathering strength and Tiphys handling the polished steering oar, the ship steadily gained speed against the contrary current. Well into the channel and past the Trojan watchers, the south wind powerfully drove the ship, allowing the men to admire the steep cliffs of the Chersonisos on the left and the flat Asian shoreline on the right. Argo moved like a coiled spring, cutting through the waves at double speed and sailing undetected past Dardania, Abydos, Perkoti, and Pityousa, all allies of mighty Troy. Then the narrow Hellespont opened into the wonderfully wide Propontis Sea. Compared to the dark strait, the Propontis was sun-filled heaven, birds chirping to Orpheus's lyre, fish breaking the water's surface in fun.

"Jason, after the ship's passage through the Hellespont, you said your Jason felt vindicated for choosing the more arduous Samothraki course. Yet at the crew's meeting, Jason remained silent, never saying a word. So what does he feel vindicated about?"

"Don't you see? Jason trusted his team to make the right decision, and when they did there was no need for him to impose his views. The crew rowed harder and longer because they made the decision rather than waiting for me to tell them what to do."

"Wait a minute! Which Jason are you? Are you the boy who's eating supper with me, or are you the Argo's courageous captain?"

"Cheiron, there's only one Jason, and I am both."

So the story-game was working, but was it working the right way? Jason was Jason, but he also thought he was Argo's captain. The story-game's aim was to simulate experience that would lodge in Jason's unconscious as if he had actually lived what he'd merely imagined. Now he said he was both boy and captain, while in fact he was only one person, not two. I wasn't sure whether he was having fun or actually believed what he said. I, for one, was determined to prevent the boy's mind from confusing the real Jason, who was thirteen years old, with the fictional Jason of the story-game.

Resuming his Argonaut persona, Jason instructed Nauplios to chart a course directly across the Propontis straight to the mouth of the Bosporos. The crew was happy and rowed with élan, hoisting and lowering the sail as the wind shifted every which way throughout the day. When the sun sank lower and daylight fled from the face of the sea, Tiphys spotted a speck of land on the horizon that, on closer inspection, turned out to be a group of isles. The largest seemed to be linked by an isthmus to the Anatolian coast. Aethalides had heard of the place and believed the island was called Arctonisos; one part of it was ruled by Kyzikos and the other by a wild Pelasgian tribe.

When Argo pulled up on Arctonisos, the Argonauts had sailed forty hours or more and badly needed a rest. Certain that the island was beyond the reach of the Trojan navy, Tiphys dropped anchor at the first suitable spot. As the crew waded ashore, they were greeted by a splendidly dressed nobleman. He was King Kyzikos, a ruler known to be eager to meet strangers from faraway lands.

Kyzikos asked Jason about Thessaly and Boeotia, and Jason inquired about the people and geography of the Propontis region. Kyzikos warned Jason about the Pelasgi, the inhabitants of the island's western part—a warlike people who ate uncooked food. Jason and Kyzikos quickly became friends, and the king invited the whole crew to visit Chytus, his fortified city, and join his people in a welcoming feast. The Hellenes and their hosts had a good time, flavored wine oiling their veins, roasted mutton filling their bellies, and amorous dreams ruffling their sleep.

Early the next morning, the Argonauts split into two groups. Jason's detachment climbed the island's Mount Didymum to get a bird's-eye view of the Propontis while Herakles, with the other half of the crew, stayed behind to guard the ship. Finding the Hellenes split in halves and Kyzikos still asleep, the Pelasgi attacked, using boulders to block the harbor and hurling stones and spears at Herakles and his men. But the Pelasgi had never met a man like Herakles before. Bending his bow and swinging his club, he quickly dispatched several of the brutes while Jason's group rushed down from the mountain and slew the rest. Pumped full of adrenalin from killing twenty-one savages, the Argonauts removed the boulders, climbed onboard, and rowed Argo out of the island's narrow port.

Propelled by a fresh breeze, the ship soon plied the waves at a fast clip, and the crew lost sight of Arctonisos in less than an hour. But as the wind gained strength, whipping the sea into vicious swirls, Tiphys had trouble keeping the ship on course, and, unable to see beyond the prow, soon lost his sense of direction. The wind roared with deadly force, like two armies clashing in battle, and with wave after wave bashing the ship, Jason thought the end was at hand, his fate to die away from home. But thanks to Tiphys's skill, as well as plenty of luck, the well-built Argo survived the day-long storm and, in barely seaworthy shape, slowly drifted toward an unknown shore.

Alas the Minyans' luck ended the moment they stepped ashore. Surprised by a barrage of arrows and spears, the ambushed shipmates were pressed to fight for their lives, hacking and thrusting, killing one foe after the other until those still alive backed off and withdrew. The Hellenes did what they did best: fight and kill, no mercy given. In truth no one could prevail against the likes of Herakles, Meleager, Peleus, and Polydeukes, who, in short order, killed thirteen of the unknown attackers without suffering a single casualty.

Then came dawn, and its waking light revealed the awful

truth: the slain foes were friends, not enemies, and Kyzikos was one of the dead. Believing the beastly Pelasgi had invaded his side of the island, Kyzikos had paid with his life for wrongly identifying Argo's crew. Kleite, the king's young wife, couldn't bear the pain of his death, and, adding sorrow to sorrow, hung herself in despair. No one openly blamed the Argonauts, but everyone knew that if they had never set foot on Arctonisos, none of this would have come to pass. Now nothing would ever be the way it was.

The people of Chytus mourned for three full days, attending the funeral pyres and playing the traditional games for the dead. But the dead stayed dead. The mourning, praying, and rivers of tears could not change what had happened; the rituals merely soothed the grief of the living. The Argonauts prayed the most because they were the instruments of Kysikos's death. But while others may have left in infamy, the Argonauts attended each of the funerals, their love of the dead outweighing the burden of their guilt.

Jason's plan was to depart after the burials, but foul weather kept the ship wind-bound for another twelve days. When the storm eventually calmed and birds resumed their normal flight, Mopsos expressed confidence that the weather had changed for good. The shipmates climbed Mount Didymum a final time, offered sacrifices to expiate their guilt, and, quite inexplicably, asked the Hellenic gods—the very same who had failed Kyzikos—for safe passage ahead. Then, dipping their oars into the water, they rowed away from the tragically diminished Arctonisos, leaving her people to an uncertain fate.

The weather completely reversed from the previous week. The fiery storm transformed into a suffocating calm; the formerly churning sea was a mirrorlike plate. As in the Bay of Melas, the crew once again was condemned to row all day under a blistering sun. With the day's heat and humidity sapping the Argonauts' spirit, the ship's progress was painfully slow and finally halted when Herakles, working hardest of all, splintered his oar. When the already exhausted crew proved unable to make up for the idled Herakles, Jason called it a day and directed Tiphys to head for the Mysian coast where the Osti River joins the Propontis Sea.

The moment Ankaeos lowered the anchor stone, Herakles rushed into the forest, looking for timber to replace his broken oar, while Hylas and Polyphemos went off seeking a spring to replenish their water skins. Within minutes Hylas cried out in distress and then fell silent. Hearing the anguished scream, Polyphemos and Herakles instantly set out to find Hylas, but, despite searching the forest all night and into the morning, were unable to find a single trace of the youth.

Meanwhile, back at the anchorage, the morning sun brought with it a stiff breeze, causing willows to sway and fir trees to creak, and urging the crew to scramble on board and unfurl the sail. With the wind at her back, Argo parted the sea like a knife cutting butter, lifting everyone's hearts in joyful relief. Alas no one noticed that Herakles, Polyphemos, and Hylas were not aboard. When Nauplios finally counted heads and found that three were missing, the ship had traveled miles from the coast. Making a return into the wind would be both difficult and costly in time. What was to be done? They had to turn back and pick up their mates, didn't they? They couldn't leave them behind, or could they? Each member of the crew asked himself the same question, but none of them dared to mouth an answer. Each blamed the other for overlooking the missing three, and each professed his empathy and deep concern. Yet no one, not Jason or Peleus or any other member of the crew, proposed to reverse course and row all the way back.

Jason's lower lip quivered when he recited the circumstances of abandoning three of his men. This was a bad tale, morally the most dubious event of the voyage to date. Philyra was visibly upset about Jason's latest phase of the story-game, particularly when she realized that Jason had passively concurred with his shipmates' reluctance to rescue the three. How could her darling Jason heartlessly forsake his friends? Was it happpenstance or subconscious intent?

Jason offered no explanation, abruptly got up, and left the cave. Philyra, turning on me, told me in no uncertain terms that playing the story-game was turning her grandson into an egotistical, vainglorious Hellene. Before playing the role of captain, Jason had been a caring and helpful boy, respectful of others' feelings and needs, whereas now, barely a year later, he was killing people by the dozens and deserted three shipmates for the sake of a stiff breeze. What kind of teaching was that? What was the story-game doing to Jason's soul?

Philyra was right: something was wrong. But it was not what she feared. When Jason had run from the cave, he'd felt anguish and plenty of guilt, more than his young heart could endure. At breakfast the following morning, he explained how the crew, rushing onboard to catch the rising wind, hadn't known that the three had gone off. Everyone had assumed the whole team was present. After weeks of calm, there was no question they had to run with the wind! No one abandoned the three on purpose, Jason was sure of that. It was a truthful account, but it was also an artful spin because Jason well knew that Herakles's overbearing persona had rubbed many the wrong way. Constantly bragging about his twelve labors, eating everyone's food to fill his gut, and hectoring the crew on Lemnos had won him no friends, and many had silently wished he were off the ship. Putting his feelings into words, his eyes welling up, Jason ruefully admitted they should have turned back but didn't because no one, including himself, wanted Herakles back onboard. What they had done was terribly wrong, but it was done, and the voyage had to go on.

All that day and the following night, Argo moved swiftly across the sea thanks to the breeze that had precipitated the ship's hasty, early morning start. With the wind doing the rowers' work, the shipmates lounged idly on deck, brooding about their abandoned friends, looking in shame at their now-empty seats. Guilt-laden gloominess hovered over the ship until another calm forced the crew to work the oars once more in search of a safe anchorage spot. For the second time in barely a month, the Argonauts stumbled on a hostile beach where they were met by a group of heavily armed men. The horde's leader was Amykos, king of the Bebrykian realm. Without a welcoming word or a courteous gesture, Amykos abruptly challenged one of the Argonauts to a one-on-one duel to the death. Keenly missing Herakles's skill, Jason hesitated to name a new champion, but gratefully acknowledged Polydeukes when he stepped forward and accepted the king's call.

Without further ado the two combatants tied on boxing gloves and commenced trading blows until Polydeukes landed a hard right above Amykos's ear, smashing his skull and killing him on the spot.

Shocked by their king's stunning defeat, the Bebrykians

rose in blind anger and recklessly attacked the unsuspecting Hellenes. But Jason's men, first unfairly challenged and then betrayed, reacted with unparalleled fury, killed four Bebrykian grunts in quick order and put the others to flight. While Iphitos was badly hurt and Talaos suffered a minor wound, Jason and the rest of the crew cherished their victory—their third straight triumph since reaching the Propontis Sea. Killing locals without losing a man was proof of their superiority, or so they thought. Proud and self-righteous, the Argonauts saw no reason to move on, and decided to spend the night at the place of their latest killings.

Krorones, who had come by for a visit, was appalled by Jason's lusty account of the Bebrykian battle. Three bloody encounters and scores of deaths were glorious only when seen through Hellenic eyes. What had become of Jason? Was he a bloodthirsty Hellene, or was he one of us? Or was he neither? His genes were Hellenic, but he had been raised by us; blood and environment had produced an uncertain mix. Thinking back I have trouble deciding who Jason was at the time— what emotions and thoughts filled his mind, and whether the story-game had made him better or worse. Nessos had noticed Jason's obsession with sacrificial rituals, Philyra was dumbstruck by his cold-blooded betrayal of friends, and now Krorones deplored his matter-of-fact attitude about killing men. What was happening to the boy's soul?

"Jason, your Argonauts have been fighting ever since you passed the Hellespont, routinely killing dozens of adversaries as if they were abstractions, not flesh-and-blood men. Why all this gruesome bloodshed? Why kill anyone at all?"

"It happened. What can I say?"

"Jason, please. You make the game—you decide what happens. Just how many men did your Jason kill?"

"He killed thirty-seven without suffering a single loss."

"You speak as if you are proud of what he did. But killing people is not a game. Each of the thirty-seven had a life until you and your men took it. Each was a husband, father, brother, or son, and now he is gone."

"Yes, I know, but their deaths weren't my fault."

"Did you or did you not set foot on other peoples' lands without their prior permission?"

"Cheiron, your argument is beside the point. You weren't with us and therefore can't possibly know what it was like to be attacked at night. If we hadn't fought back, we would all be dead. Is that what you want?"

Philyra was right: Jason had become a heartless killing machine. It was kill first and ask questions later, if he asked any questions at all. Empathy was a thing of the past; what mattered was getting to Kolchis. All else was means to that end. The story-game had turned nasty, and exceedingly so, but so was life, and the game's purpose was to prepare Jason for the world as it was. But life had other dimensions as well, such as friendship and love, kindness and charity, justice and truth, and the story-game had to find a place for them too. In rushing the ship toward Kolchis, Jason had given life's virtues short shrift. What the story-game needed was a morally positive experience.

Early the next morning, on the thirty-first day of the voyage, Jason roused the crew from deep sleep and urged them to wash up, eat, and get ready to go. Jason was worried: with Iphitos seriously wounded; Herakles, Polyphemos, and Hylas gone; Tiphys steering the ship; and Orpheus calling the beat, the rowing contingent was down to twenty-four men—barely enough to propel the galley through the turbulent waters of the Bosporos. The channel was only eighteen miles long and eight hundred yards wide at its narrowest point—much narrower than the Hellespont. The narrowness sharply accelerated the flow of the water and created an extremely powerful down-current, making it impossible to row a galley upstream even with a favorable wind at her back. However, the very speed of the down-current engendered small countercurrents near the channel's banks, where water flowed backward, filling gaps caused by the suction of the downstream-rushing current. These countercurrents, close to the channel's sides and difficult to spot, were the only practical way to row a ship up the Bosporos.

Within minutes of leaving the Bebrykian shore, the ship was pummeled and tossed by the rough waters of the Bosporos Strait. Wave after onrushing wave pounded Argo's hull, threatening to capsize the ship. Her wooden planks creaked in pain. The roar of the current drowned Orpheus's music, obliging the singer to shout his stroke count over the wind. Ignoring common sense, Tiphys set a course straight across the channel, hoping to locate a countercurrent on the western bank. With no room for error, the crew rowed at full strength for well over an hour when, within yards of the European side, the water suddenly changed from uncontrolled fury to an irregularly moving counterflow that allowed the shipmates to row upstream. The countercurrent prevailed for several miles before it began to weaken and then disappeared.

Reasoning that the countercurrent had switched to the channel's opposite side, Tiphys ordered the crew to traverse the Bosporos a second time. Trusting him with their lives, the

Argonauts put hands to oars, confident they would make it safely across, as they had before.

Tiphys was right: there was a backward-flowing current on the eastern bank that allowed the crew to row upstream with relative ease for about four miles. When that current eventually faded, Tiphys steered the ship across the channel for a third time and then cast anchor on the western bank. Exhausted to their bones' marrow, and too tired to eat, the men fell to the ground where they stood, and within seconds sank into sleep. The Bosporos, however, was of a different mettle. Its powerful current continued to rush down the channel nonstop, tumbling from rock to shore with frightening force.

When morning's first light softened the sky, Jason awakened his tired crew for another day of battle against the hellish Bosporos. Tiphys loosened the hawsers; the men fitted oars to tholes and gently eased the ship into the countercurrent's upstream drift. Alas the countercurrent lasted less than a mile, and the crew had to recross the channel again. Then it was back to the European side for the last time. Rowing at a measured pace, and carefully staying within the narrow band of the backward-flowing current, Argo reached the northern entrance to the Bosporos as night began to fall. With the sun retired after a full day's work and rain-heavy clouds hiding the stars, Jason opted to anchor Argo in a small cove protected by sheer cliffs. The place was Gyropolis, so named after the numerous buzzards and gulls that nested in the cove's steeply rising palisades.

The Argonauts beached their ship, set up camp, and, while reconnoitering the immediate environs, stumbled on an emaciated man sprawled across the doorway of a ramshackle hut. Was he dead or alive? And who might he be? Nude and incredibly filthy, his eye sockets empty, the creature stunk to heaven, but he was not dead! Hearing the Argonauts' footsteps, the man raised his head, saying his name was Phineus. But why was he here and in such miserable shape?

Anxious to solicit the Argonauts' help, Phineus told the sad story of his overly long life—how as king he had led his people from Thraki to Bithynia, how his second marriage had torn his family apart, and, adding insult to injury, how he had lost his throne. He was blind, poor, and banished to this cove. The birds now dictated his life, eating all his food and shitting on him for fun.

The shipmates were appalled, pity warming their battle-hardened hearts. Zetes and Kalais promised to rid the cove of its birds, Talaos cooked Phineus a meal, and Telamon cleaned the old man. But, as the meal was served, flocks of cormorants and gulls dived from the sky and snatched every morsel of food. Incensed, Zetes and Kalais climbed the escarpment with drawn knives, destroying every egg and killing every chick they could reach. The vultures watched in horror as their young were exterminated, but no one pitied the birds; everyone's empathy was reserved for Phineus alone. Within an hour every single nest was destroyed and the vultures, robbed of home and offspring, flew off in search of another place. Telamon finished washing the filth off Phineus while Jason and Eribotes sacrificed a sheep in the old king's honor. Free of birds, sated and clean, Phineus was only too eager to tell all he knew about the sea route to Kolchis.

Philyra listened raptly to Jason's tale of the Phineus encounter. For once the Argonauts didn't kill the first man they met upon beaching their ship, but selflessly helped a person who couldn't help himself. Philyra had hoped for the story-game to feature such an experience, and it finally did.

"Jason, why did you help poor Phineus, a seemingly useless old man?"

"Philyra, he was dying, and we had to know what he knew."

"Well, did you help him out of pity, or because you thought he might be of use?"

"What difference does it make? Helping Phineus benefited us and him. Everyone was better off as a result of what we did."

Philyra sadly shook her head. She had hoped for Jason to act out of charity, not engage in a premeditated act intended to benefit the expedition. Yet her judgment seemed overly harsh. As Jason told the story, the men gave Phineus a helping hand before they learned of his identity. And the shipmates' first reactions were genuinely unselfish—different from the subsequent sacrifice of a sheep, which was calculated to gain Phineus's trust. But if Jason and his men weren't perfect Samaritans, their treatment of Phineus was a mile-high improvement over their wholesale killings on Arctonisos and Bebrykia.

With the birds chased away, the cove turned peacefully quiet, imparting a long and restful night to Phineus and his new friends. Alas, on the following morning, the Etesian winds commenced their annual forty-day exercise of blowing furiously from east to west, making the sea totally unsafe. Anxious to make use of their idle time, Jason encouraged Nauplios and Tiphys to befriend Phineus and learn from him all he knew about the Euxine Sea. Phineus, grateful for the Argonauts' help, was only too eager to pontificate about Argo's best route. After crossing the northern mouth of the Bosporos, Argo was to sail eastward and parallel to the Euxine Sea's southern coast, all the way to Kolchis—a target impossible to miss. The whole trip would take between thirty and sixty days depending on weather conditions. The ship would pass by the mouth of the Rhebas River, circumvent the Black Cape, come to the island of Thynias, sail past the Carambis foreland, and meet the mighty Halys River. Farther east would be Cape Themiskyra, the river Thermodon, an island off the Messyneeci coast, and finally the marshes at the mouth of the Phasis River.

"Jason, how do you know these Asian place names? They are news to me."

"Phineus told me. He knows the Euxine well."

"Jason, don't be absurd. Whatever Phineus says are words you put into his mouth. So how did you know what Phineus said?"

"I know what Phineus said because I heard him say it."

"Yes, Jason. In the story-game you are Argo's captain, and Phineus tells you how to get from Gyropolis to Kolchis. But at this moment in time, you are not on the Euxine Sea. Rather you are standing next to me in front of the cave where we both live. So I expect an answer from you, not from your story-game alter ego."

"All right, if you have to know, Krorones told me about the Euxine and the way to Kolchis. He also told me about King Aietes, the wily ruler of Kolchis. Cheiron, to be perfectly honest, I am not sure I can do it."

"Not sure you can do what?"

"I can't be Jason and Aietes at the same time. They are opponents and entirely different men. One is a young adventurer, the other is an authoritarian king. I can't be both at the same time!"

"Jason, don't tell me you want to quit the game."

"No, I want to continue, but not alone. I have been doing all the work while you have done nothing. Why don't you play a part too? Why can't you be Aietes?"

Had I known then what would happen later, I would have declined Jason's request, but his entreaty seemed reasonable enough, and so I acquiesced. The Argonauts' plan was to plunder Kolchis, and Aietes would do what he could to protect his gold. Playing Aietes would require me to pretend I was a foreign king defending his wealth, which didn't seem difficult at all. Chariklo, however, who had joined us for supper that night, saw Jason's idea in an entirely different light, insisting that my playing Aietes was pitting father against son. Alas the die was cast: I could not disappoint Jason by retracting my earlier assent. Henceforth I would be both Cheiron of Pelion and King Aietes of Kolchis.

After forty days the Etisian winds abated, and the weather cleared up. The Argonauts gathered their gear and prepared to depart, but found it heartbreakingly difficult to bid Phineus goodbye. Standing by the readied ship, Phineus gave his new-found friends detailed instructions on how to navigate the clashing rocks at the Bosporos's northern gate. His dead eyes fixed on the distant horizon, Phineus explained that a mile or so north the countercurrent would pull the ship through an area of half-submerged rocks. The large, clumpy rocks would be easily visible, but unpredictable wind gusts whipping around the headland would make it difficult to control the ship. The prudent course of action was to wait for an intermittent moment when the winds were relatively calm. Phineus counseled to test the wind's force by releasing a dove, and follow her path provided her flight was even and straight. Then Phineus said farewell and turned away.

For a final time, the backward flow of the countercurrent moved the ship north, requiring only minimal help from the men's oars. The Argonauts soon sighted the swirling waters around the dark-colored rocks, and, after waiting for a suitably calm moment, released a dove. When the bird's flight traced a straight line between the rocks, Jason called on the men to row with all their strength, bending their oars like crossbows and driving the ship at maximum speed before any suddenly rising gusts could smash the ship against the rocks. Orpheus, setting aside his lyre, shouted the stroke count over the noise of the swirling sea while Tiphys deftly steered the galley between the wave-clashed rocks. When the ship was through, the vastness of the Euxine Sea stretched out ahead like freedom from prison, and the crew broke out in hoary cheers, celebrating their deed. Then Tiphys reset the steering blade on an easterly course, directing Argo to sail parallel to Anatolia's northern shore.

Healthy and fresh after their long sojourn at Gyropolis, the Argonauts rowed like oxen plowing the earth, quickly passing the rivers Rhebas and Phyllis before entering Thynias Island's snug, natural harbor at dawn the next day. But when the men stepped ashore, their confidence went poof. For the first time since the voyage had begun, the men found themselves in a strangely scary world—strange because they were in Asia, scary because they were in the Euxine Sea. Far from home, far from anything they knew, the Minyans lost their inner bearings and, frightened by their fear, fell back on their silly religion and built an altar to Zeus, sacrificed another sheep, and swore a mutual brotherhood oath.

The oath was Idmon's idea. The men were afraid of the Euxine but also of each other, not knowing what each would do under duress. Their minds were wrapped in dread, non-specific and undefined; fear of the unknown engulfed the ship. Jason was no exception. His mood was depressed; his demeanor had soured, and he projected the opposite of inspiration. Spooked like his crew, Jason repeatedly delayed leaving the safety of Thynias, ignoring the call of the Kolchian quest. Phineus's prediction of smooth sailing gave him no comfort at all, for how could an old man's dead eyes determine a future event? The future could be anything at all, ranging from good to bad and worse. Anything could happen in the Euxine Sea.

Tiphys alone, secure in his seamanship, confidently shrugged off his comrades' fears of rough weather, triple waves, sea monsters, hostile gods, or whatever scared them out of their wits. But Jason still dithered for three whole days, unwilling to leave Thynias's safe harbor until, finally, a rising fresh breeze forced his decision. The whole crew knew full well that the voyage was over unless Argo followed the wind. Goaded by Peleus and Tiphys, the men reluctantly embarked, unfurled the sail, and left Thynias Island behind. Thereafter the ship made excellent time, splendidly riding the waves. The wind held all day and far into the night before falling off when Argo came within sight of Cape Acherusias. Not wishing to round the treacherous point in the dark, Jason decided to beach the ship before night gave way to day.

Answering one of Philyra's manifold questions, Jason described his transient irresolution as a glob of blackness that had invaded his mind. Was he depressed or bewitched by dark omens? Was the story-game the source of Jason's black mood?

Not really, I thought. While the game postulated events to simulate experience, Jason's depression seemed unrelated to any experience, occurring solely in the boy's mind. He had delayed leaving Thynias not because his Jason had been frightened but because he had been uncertain how to plan the story-game's next phase.

Dropping anchor near Cape Acherusias in Mariandynia, the Argonauts received a truly warm welcome from King Lykus and his people, who loudly cheered the arriving crew, embraced the men when they stepped ashore, and profusely thanked them for killing Amykos. The Bebrykians had harassed the Mariandyni for many years, until the day when Polydeukes had smashed Amykos's skull and put his henchman to flight. Ever since Mariandynia had been at peace, people no longer feared for their lives, and prosperity ruled the land. Grateful beyond belief, the Mariandyni proclaimed Polydeukes their national hero and invited the whole crew to visit the royal palace at Heraklea. King Lykus, intent on expressing his gratitude, also proposed that his son Daskylos join Argo's depleted crew—an offer Jason was happy to accept. Argonauts and Mariandyni feasted on sweet tuna and swordfish, and drank gallons of beer until midnight, when Jason thanked King Lykus for his hospitality and announced that Argo would sail at dawn.

But fate's cruel hand made naught of Jason's plans. As the sun rose the next day and the men made their way to the ship, brave Idmon was mortally gored by a boar. Hearing his desperate plea for help, Telamon and Meleagros rushed to his side and killed the boar, but Idmon was beyond help and died in the arms of his friends. Jason told the shipmates of Idmon's death, and they reacted with incredulity. They understood what Jason was saying, but failed to process his words' content. Less than five minutes earlier, Idmon had been fooling around at breakfast, breaking an egg on Mopsos's bald head. And now he was dead? How was that possible? It was unreasonable for Idmon to be killed by a mindless beast!

But while Idmon's death made no earthly sense, his corpse was an undeniable fact, leaving the Argonauts no choice but to mourn for the customary three days and bury Idmon on the fourth. Yet death was not finished, striking a second time when valiant Tiphys caught a fever that brought him down. Two funerals in a week were more than the shipmates could bear; grief gripped their hearts, and a bewildered Jason questioned the point of the voyage.

"Cheiron, I don't get it. Every time there's a problem, Jason implies that his Jason doesn't want to go on. What's his issue? Has he lost faith in the voyage? Or is he tired of playing the game?"

"Nessos, I am puzzled the same as you, but I don't believe Jason is quitting the game. He asked me only this morning who I thought should take Tiphys's place."

"What was your advice?"

"I said the decision was his."

"So what's his problem?"

"Jason is struggling with *nam-us*—what it means and why it happens. His friend Dryas died last week, and Jason cried through the night, pouring his heart out to Chariklo, who had come over for supper. He said Dryas's death was unfair, that Dryas had done nothing wrong, and he questioned the purpose of life if death can end it at will. When Chariklo explained that death is merely the end of life, not any kind of retribution or punishment, Jason replied that if life is as she says, why should any man do anything other than wait until death knocks at the gate?"

"Did Dryas die before or after Jason had Idmon killed by that boar?"

"Nessos, you guessed it."

Each person, at one time or other, must face the fact that life is finite—that it has a beginning and an end. Jason knew about death, but it was something that happened to others, not to him or anyone he knew. When Dryas died, a boy his own age, Jason was shocked that it would someday also happen to him. Death no longer was an abstraction; it had become reality, an ugly, unavoidable fact. Jason, of course, was right in calling death absurd and arbitrary, because that is exactly the nature of death. But he was wrong saying death robs life of meaning. If humans were immortal, life would surely be different, but the meaning of life wouldn't much differ from the life we have. One thing, however, seemed fairly clear: brooding about death wasn't doing Jason much good, and the cure was not to give him a lecture but to coax him back into the game.

"Jason, who did you appoint as Tiphys's replacement?"

"The choice was between Ankaeos, Erginos, Euphemos, and Nauplios—all capable of steering the ship, though none as qualified as Tiphys."

"So who did you pick?"

"The men chose Ankaeos."

With Tiphys buried and Ankaeos taking his place, Jason had planned to leave right after the funerals, but bad weather kept the ship stranded another three days. When a stiff breeze finally blew from the west, the Argonauts embarked in a flash, stowed their gear, and pushed off from the beach. Staying any longer would have ossified their sorrow, their mode of mourning lapsing into morbid depression. Indeed, for Jason's mind to stay healthy and bold, it was high time for him to resume command of the living and forget about death.

Ankaeos grasped the steering blade, Daskylos took Idmon's seat, and the crew rowed the ship away from the shore, quickly unfurling the wind-catching sail. Ankaeos was excellent at steering the ship from point to point while fighting an occasional three-step wave along the way. Sailing parallel to Anatolia's coast, the Argonauts made a short stop at Lyra, sailed on through the night, and passed Cape Carambis at sunrise the following day.

When the sea turned choppy and the wind grew uncommonly fickle—blowing hard, then calm, then coming in gusts—Jason saw Ankaeos struggling to keep the ship on course and wisely decided to make landfall at Sinopi, the northernmost point of the Anatolian coast. Some years earlier Herakles had punished three of his soldiers by banishing them to this place. Longing to return home, the three now tearfully begged to join Argo's team, and Jason gladly took them aboard.

Not long after leaving Sinopi, a strong northwestern breeze drove Argo past several rivers—first Halys, then Iris, and, after rounding Cape Themiskyra, the fabled Thermodon. Approaching the mouth of the Thermodon River, Jason surmised the coastline to be part of the Amazons' territory. Weren't the Amazons archenemies of Hellas, and wasn't this a perfect opportunity to avenge the deaths of Tiphys and Idmon and conduct proper funeral games for his dear friends? Without revealing his intent, Jason ordered Ankaeos to make landfall and drop anchor forthwith. The shipmates jumped off not knowing where they were, but grateful to stretch their stiff legs.

However, the moment the Argonauts stepped on shore, hundreds of well-armed Amazons lined up in battle formation, ready to teach the Minyans a lesson. The crew was totally unprepared and badly outnumbered. Jason took one look at the opposing force, found it prudent to beat a hasty retreat, and ordered the men to row out to sea safely beyond reach of the Amazons' spears.

When I asked Jason why he made landfall at the one place where he was certain to face hostility, he said he was doing what he had done all along, which was to go onshore whenever the crew ran out of provisions or was too tired to go on. Shaking my head in disbelief, Jason clamped his lips, not saying another word. He wasn't embarrassed, and didn't play coy, but his silence suggested he had landed on Themiskyra with a different purpose in mind. The purpose, I guessed, was to take prisoners to avenge the deaths of Idmon and Tiphys. What was the boy thinking? Did he believe the capture and sacrifice of a dozen Amazons would help his dead friends? But that's how the Hellenes think: tit for tat, although killing prisoners in honor of a slain friend is no honor at all and does nothing for the dead. Jason, my dear son, was thinking more and more like a typical Hellene. It was time we had a serious talk.

"Jason, are you still mourning Idmon and Tiphys?"

"I do. They were my friends, and they weren't properly buried."

"Says who?"

"Pholos told me how the Hellenes lament their dead, and since Idmon and Tiphys were Hellenes, I wanted to do the same for them."

"Jason, I understand, but Pholos's advice is wrong. Your friends are dead, and killing prisoners won't bring them back. What's more, Idmon and Tiphys didn't die in battle, and you have no prisoners of war. You can't just invade a place, capture a handful of people, and cut their throats because Pholos says it is a Hellenic tradition. Don't listen to Pholos. He talks without knowing what he is talking about."

"But I'm still angry. Their deaths were unfair."

"What are you saying?"

"Kolchis is yet to come."

The sea route from the Bosporos to Kolchis runs roughly eight hundred miles—an enormous distance for a small crew to row a wooden ship, miles and miles of rowing, hours and days of ennui and mind-numbing work. It took ninety-one days for the Argonauts to sail from Gyropolis to the Thermodon River—ninety-one days of backbreaking labor, blistery hands, and painfully aching arms and legs. Jason, who had never rowed a boat or set foot on a galley before, took his crew's labors for granted. He was unable to appreciate fully their herculean task. Rowing the ship was backbreaking hard and deadly monotonous, and worst of all it never seemed to end. The Argonauts' normal pace was four strokes per minute, two hundred and forty strokes per hour, and half a million strokes for the whole distance from Iolkos to Kolchis. And the rowing stroke was always the same: faster in times of danger or heavy seas, slower or resting with a following wind, but always end-lessly repetitive, always the same identical motion of dipping the blade into the water and pulling it through, again and again and again.

The muscles engaged in rowing consume most of the body's oxygen, leaving less for the organs, thus causing fatigue. When at sea oarsmen cannot rest, but are compelled to row or risk endangering the ship. The Argonauts' commitment to the voyage was a commitment to row, and once at sea the men had no choice but to honor their obligation in full. The men understood their duty, but they also felt trapped and weren't happy about any of it. And their unhappiness grew as the voyage dragged on. Jason knew something was wrong, but never having rowed himself, didn't know what troubled the men.

An hour after the Argonauts escaped the Amazons, the wind faded and died. Orpheus reached for his lyre and started to sing an old song, compelling the crew once again to row to his beat. But the rowing was ragged; few of the men pulled their oars as required, and a palpable discontent settled over the ship. Why had they joined this confounded voyage? Why this commitment to endless work? Wouldn't they rather die in battle than collapse pulling their oars?

Watching his men grow listless and weak, Jason urged Orpheus to rev up his singing, although Jason knew that even the best song gets boring when heard for the fiftieth time. Boredom is the child of monotony and can be as deadly as death, but the condition is not hopeless if deconstructed and reset into a positive mode. Jason, however, had no clue what to do while his crew's morale was sinking to the point of no return.

Philyra poured grape juice into Jason's ceramic cup and consolingly stroked his matted hair, wondering whether he was
getting a cold or—knock on wood—whether his old illness
had reappeared. Jason denied he was ill, but, with tears suddenly flooding his eyes, confessed the story-game was just
about over because the Argonauts were tired and wanted to
go home. He said he didn't know how to revitalize the crew
and insisted he couldn't ask me because, in my role as Aietes,
I wasn't supposed to know how badly demoralized his men
really were. Instead Jason reached out to Philyra and also
to Chariklo, asking them what he should do. Having been a
goatherd for years, Chariklo was no stranger to boredom and
monotony. Her advice was for Jason to challenge his men with
a difficult task—one that was both dangerous and physically
demanding. Facing the possibility of pain and failure would be
like a wake-up call, forcing the men to abandon their apathetic
attitude.

Racking his brain for a suitable challenge, Jason remembered
old Phineus referring to Ares, a windswept island rock that was
home to thousands of nasty birds. Jason had no idea whether
Phineus's story was fantasy or fact, or whether the birds could
inflict serious pain, but he thought a side trip to Ares, a mile
and a half off the coast, may well break the monotony that
paralyzed the Argonauts' will. His mind made up, Jason
relieved Ankaeos at the helm and surreptitiously steered Argo
out to sea.

Before long a giant seagull circled the ship, suddenly dived
low, and released a feather that, like a sharp-pointed arrow,
pierced Oileus's muscled chest. More birds arrived, hundreds
of them, all shrieking and flapping their wings, flying low and

aiming not only their feathers at the startled men but also their foul-smelling dung. Phineus had been right: the birds of Ares were deadly; the Argonauts were in for a fight.

If the birds weren't enough, the wind gained strength and threatened to tear the sail into shreds. The men managed to brail up barely before the gusts became gales, forcing Jason to moor the ship on the rocky isle. To keep the birds at bay, a dozen of the shipmates formed a panoply with their shields while the rest of the crew rowed to keep the ship upright and dry. When the galley at last neared stark Ares and came to rest on a rocky ledge, the men yelled at the top of their voices and loudly banged their shields, hoping to scare off the birds. The vultures had never heard such ungodly noise before. Bewildered, the birds rose high in the air and, screeching like monkeys, left Ares behind.

Exhausted from rowing the ship through the gale, the shipmates were gratified and proud of having defeated both the birds and the sea. Exerting a maximum effort had filled their brains with endorphin and caused their egos to brim with confidence. The sea was still angry, with storm gusts lashing the anchored ship, but the men were safe, and their spirits were up as they watched the wild tumbles of the Euxine Sea's feared triple waves. Looking out at the murderous sea, Euphemos suddenly spotted four desperately struggling men clinging to a large, wooden plank. Mountain-high waves played cat and mouse with the poor souls, and Peleus wagered Mopsos whether the four would drown or make it to Ares alive. A huge wave settled the issue as the four were forcefully swept ashore in a giant, watery whoosh.

The Argonauts pulled the four from the water and wrapped them in whatever blankets were at hand. The shipwrecked men said their homeland was Kolchis, and they had been sailing to Hellas when the storm sunk their ship. Their father's name was Phrixos, though he was no longer alive; their mother was Chalkiope, King Aietes's oldest child. With their ship destroyed and their only choice to continue on foot, they respectfully asked Jason to ferry them to the mainland after the storm. Jason, however, had other thoughts. He considered the four brothers welcome additions to his short-manned crew, and furthermore figured they could be useful guides when entering Kolchis. So he replied that he would be glad to take them all the way to Hellas, but before heading home he intended to pay King Aietes a visit.

Alas going back to Kolchis was not what the four had in mind, and they told Jason that calling on Aietes would be a colossal mistake. Didn't Jason know their grandfather's reputation, his absolute refusal to admit any foreigners to his domain? Aietes mistrusted anyone not born in Kolchis, convinced that all strangers were scheming to steal his gold. The four brothers insisted Kolchis was a trap the Argonauts should avoid at all cost. But Jason's mind was made up, and he repeated his offer to take them to Hellas provided they first accompanied him and his men to their native land. The brothers' choice was brutally simple: either accept Jason's offer or be left on Ares, possibly forever. They did what they had to do.

During the night the storm gradually eased, waning from violent to gentle as dawn opened the new day. When the press-ganged four stepped onboard, their added weight caused the ship to settle low in the water and impaired Argo's maneuverability. Jason brushed aside Ankaeos's worry, arguing that four additional oarsmen would allow rowing in shifts. And Jason was right. Rowing with intermittent pauses turned out to be a big success, boosting the crew's already more-positive attitude and giving the ship extra speed. Sailing farther from home than any Hellenic ship had before, Argo passed beaches blackened by iron, villages of wooden houses, wide forest expanses, and snow-covered, distant mountaintops. Yet no matter how monotonous the Euxine landscape was, the crew rowed on in good spirits and broke out in a lusty cheer when, eight days after pushing off from Ares, the Caucasus Mountains came into view. Now Kolchis was near. Two more days of working the oars and the ship would reach the Phasis River, fabled to carry tiny bits of gold in its muddy water.

Krorones and Chariklo, his daughter and my soon-to-be wife, came over for supper that night. I had killed a boar, and Philyra had been roasting pork chops all afternoon. We talked about our forthcoming wedding, who to invite and what to serve, and Chariklo toured the cave, trying to decide where to make our home. I was thirty-two at the time, the right age for a man to get married, but Chariklo, at eighteen, was two years over the traditional age. Krorones was as taciturn as ever, looking alert but preferring to keep his mouth shut. Jason also was noticeably quiet. The boy had done an excellent job spinning the story-game all the way from Iolkos to Kolchis, but now that the Argonauts were almost there, he showed little joy and, if anything, appeared somewhat tense—worried perhaps about Aietes, with whom he was about to cross swords.

As for myself, well, I too was in a pensive mood. Marriage was a big step. No more solitary excursions down the mountain, no more nights out with Nessos, Bienor or Elatos. I loved Chariklo with all my heart, but actually being married was a sobering thought. Krorones sensed my anxiety and said not to worry; everything would work out fine with Jason. Chariklo liked Jason very much, and Krorones was sure everyone in the new family would get along fine. I thought Krorones meant well, but his concern was misplaced. Jason was not the problem, certainly not in any perceptible way. I was the problem: my doubts and misgivings about my upcoming marriage, and also my role as stand-in for Aietes.

Philyra had prepared a lovely meal, the pork chops were perfectly roasted while preserving the meat's moisture and taste. Jason ate with gusto, and between bites told us how Ankaeos was steering the ship north toward the marsh-infested Phasis estuary. The Argonauts were happy to have reached the end of their journey while Phrixos's four sons were visibly nervous about what lay ahead. Argus, the oldest of the four, urged lowering the stroke count and rowing in virtual silence, but Jason was unwilling to dampen the men's spirits and delayed heeding caution until Argo came within sight of the river. When the ship neared the mainland, Jason told Argus to take over the helm, ordered the oarsmen to hold water, and rolled up the sail to be less visible from the coast. As darkness descended and heavy clouds covered the moon and the stars, Argus asked for total silence while the ship ever so slowly moved upstream in the mud-brown Phasis River. With the men rowing long strokes, Argo glided silently along the river's western bank until Nauplios found a well-hidden mooring place in the middle of the reedy marsh. Ankaeos dumped two heavy anchor stones onto the river's bottom, and the crew retired to catch a wink of sleep before confronting Aietes the next day.

MEDEIA

Early the next morning, when the sun's rose-colored fingers lit the pale sky, Jason called his men into council to plan the conquest of Aietes's gold. To understand the Kolchian government, Jason requested that Argus describe the power of the king, the role of the nobles, and the finances of the state. Argus was flattered and launched into a lengthy discourse about gold mining and Kolchis's wealth. The yellow metal was gained in two ways: Near Sakradessi in the mountains, miners dug tunnels in search of gold-bearing veins, extracted the rocks, and separated the gold from useless stone. Down in the flatlands, sheep fleeces were placed in various streams to capture tiny flecks of gold washed down from the mountains up north. All gold mines and gold-carrying streamlets were controlled by Aietes, while the mined gold was held at the state treasury and protected by the palace guards.

King Aietes was head of the royal family and the country's legitimate ruler, but his real power was based on controlling the state treasury's gold. The royal family included Aietes; his wife, Eidyia; his children, Chalkiope, Apsyrtos, and Medeia; and

Perses, the king's younger brother. Chalkiope was the widow of Phrixos and the mother of Argus and his three brothers, Apsyrtos was the illegitimate son of Aietes and Asterodeia, and Medeia, the youngest, was the daughter of Aietes and his queen.

But the royal family was a family only in name, sharing the same forebear but little else. Aietes ruled with an iron fist, yet was old and ailing and not expected to live many more months. Spurred on by the king's declining health, his wife, his brother, and his power-hungry daughter and son feverishly schemed to take Aietes's place. Chalkiope had no interest in politics, but Apsyrtos, commander of the palace guards, was hotly ambitious and not shy about letting everyone know that he was next in line. Medeia was as power-driven as her brother but pretended to appear disinterested while building support among the common folk. The third faction vying for the throne was Queen Eidyia and Perses, the head of the army, who was favored by the landed nobility.

In Kolchis, gold and power were two sides of the same coin. All wanted gold because it could be exchanged for anything anyone wanted. The Hittite and Thrakian mercenaries were paid in gold; wheat was bought with gold from the Scythians; iron was exchanged with Chalybes for gold; and slaves could be bought for less than a grain of the metal. The royal family had everything they could possibly want, yet still sought more gold because it brought power and the means to usurp the throne. With gold and succession inextricably linked, the royals' internecine quarrel seemed destined to become a fight to the death.

Listening to Argus's words, Jason traded looks with Mopsos, wondering whether the Argonauts could use the rift among the royal family as a means to steal the gold. Jason's impulse was to storm the state treasury, while Mopsos argued that diplomacy should first be given a chance. After intense discussion the shipmates agreed to use a ruse—or call it a lie—in approaching the king. They would present themselves as highly skilled mercenaries and offer their services to the Kolchian state. A three-man delegation consisting of Jason, Augeias, and Telamon would negotiate with Aietes. The group, together with Argus and his brothers, would depart to the king's palace at once.

Taking Jason to school the next day, I broached the subjects of walking in on the Kolchian court, his audience with Aietes, whether the king would see him at all, and what his reaction would be.

"Jason, to be perfectly frank, seeing Aietes with only two companions seems reckless and foolish. You know he has killed foreigners on sight."

"I know, Cheiron, I know, but approaching Aietes as suppliants makes him subject to the guest friendship code, which means he can't harm us. What's more, Argus will testify that we saved him and his brothers."

"Well, perhaps you are right, but what will you say is your reason for coming to Kolchis? Aietes hates people who try to sneak in."

"That's exactly why we are not sneaking in but offering our services to the king."

"Jason, get real. What services can you credibly offer? Aietes is nobody's fool."

"Aietes has trouble with the Sauromatians in the north. I will offer to go up to the border and take care of his problem once and for all. He has a similar deal with the Hittites who protect his western frontier. Let me ask you: would you accept my offer if you were in Aietes's shoes?"

"Aietes will question whether Argo's crew is up to the task."

"I won't tell him how many we are. He'll only meet Augeias, Telamon, and me, not anyone else. It doesn't matter if Aietes thinks we are naïve, stupid, or incompetent as long as he believes we are suppliants looking for work. I want him to think he can use us so we can use him."

Walking at a steady pace past dense forests and across beautifully planted fields, Jason's group sighted a cluster of large buildings farther ahead. Partially obscured by the morning mist, the buildings were grouped around an immense square ringed by a high wall, which was interspersed by three solid double gates. For an instant or two, Jason stood in awe, admiring Aietes's magnificent palace, which was more glorious than any royal house back home. But remembering his task at hand, Jason's reverie was short-lived, and, gathering his wits, he resolutely strode onto the palace grounds. Astonishing as it seemed, there were no guards at the palace gates; anyone could walk in, anyone at all, permitting Jason's group to enter the courtyard completely unchallenged.

Medeia and Chalkiope, sipping tea on the palace terrace, first noticed Jason's group striding across the plaza and broke into shouts of joy when they recognized Argus and his brothers. Chalkiope rushed forward to embrace her sons while Medeia stood back, eying the strangers, whose blond hair and fair skin reminded her of Phrixos, her nephews' late father. Argus formally made the introductions while Jason stared at Medeia, and she demurely looked at him. He was startled by her delicate beauty while she was captivated by his princely pose. It was love at first sight, and in one heavenly instant their hearts skipped a beat.

The commotion in the courtyard quickly attracted attention. Royal attendants greeted the unexpected visitors while servants set up a banquet welcoming the brothers and their friends. Jason was greatly relieved that his party was offered a meal, the traditional gesture of welcoming guests. In time the Kolchians' goodwill was bound to fray, but for the moment Jason was happy to be treated as a guest rather than as a hostile invader.

When King Aietes inquired about the purpose of Jason's visit, Argus and his brothers spoke of their shipwreck and fortunate rescue by the Argonauts, while Jason explained his intention to serve the king against the Sauromatians. Aietes, suspicious by nature, wanted to know the reason behind the Hellenes' unusual request, given that no one, not a single soul, had ever volunteered to fight the fierce Sauromatians. Jason replied that soldiering was his profession, warring his livelihood, and he expected to be paid in gold.

The moment Jason mentioned gold, he knew he had made a mistake. Aietes, who had been reasonably civil until then, angrily rose from his throne, accused Jason of trying to steal his treasure, and cursed Argus and his brothers for bringing these Hellenic liars to Kolchis. Aietes said Phrixos had taught him long ago that the Hellenes were a backward people who worked with primitive plows and fought with weapons of bronze. What good are men, Aietes asked, who don't know how to farm and who don't have weapons of iron? All they could do was plunder and steal!

When Jason angrily retorted that his shipmates weren't just anybody, but sons and grandsons of the immortal gods, Aietes laughed out loud, saying the Hellenes were the only people on earth who deluded themselves to be descended from gods. Aietes's repartee left Jason at a loss for words: No one had ever questioned that Ankaeos was Poseidon's son or that Zeus had fathered Polydeukes. How could Jason convince Aietes of the Argonauts' superior abilities when the Kolchian king rejected their genealogy?

Words would not convince Aietes, that much seemed certain, but knowing that deeds speak louder than words, Jason challenged Aietes to test his skills in farming and in war. Aietes laughed aloud a second time, and with undisguised glee immediately accepted Jason's suggestion. He proposed that Jason prove his expertise as both farmer and warrior by passing two tests: one plowing and seeding a four-acre field with a Kolchian plow, the other fighting hand to hand against equal numbers of Kolchian guards. Flashing his trademark evil smile, Aietes declared that the prize for plowing the field would be a golden fleece, while winning the hand-to-hand combat would earn Jason a commission to pacify the Sauromatian people.

Paying close attention to Aietes's terms, Jason thought the proposed tests were fair, and consequently accepted the challenge. He courteously thanked Aietes and his family for their reception, and together with Augeias and Telamon left the palace to return to the ship. Needless to say Jason's confidence was sadly misplaced. All who witnessed Aietes's wording of the tests knew that Jason had been tricked, and that his chances of surviving the trials were close to nil. Chalkiope was particularly upset by the turn of events, fearing Aietes would also punish her sons for bringing the Hellenes to Kolchis. Thinking on her feet, she asked Argus to follow Jason secretly and advise him what Aietes was planning to do.

Argus caught up with Jason and his companions near the forest at the edge of the fields. Jason laughed at Argus's troubled expression, suggesting he had eaten too much mutton at the palace reception. But Argus grimly shook his head and patiently explained the severity of Aietes's tests: The farming test would require Jason to handle a new-fangled plow that was pulled not by oxen but by two fiery bulls that had killed each assigned plowman in the past. And the hand-to-hand combat would be heavily skewed in Aietes's favor; he would field equal numbers of his Hittite and Thrakian guards, rather than a number equal to the Argonauts. At first Jason couldn't believe what Argus was saying, but as he recalled the sequence of Aietes's responses, he realized he had fallen into a deadly trap. Instead of tricking Aietes into hiring him, Aietes had tricked him into tests he was certain to lose. Jason blamed himself bitterly for his arrogant carelessness. He had badly failed his crew! Would the men trust him again? Would they stay and fight or take flight in the dead of night?

Rattled to the core by fear and remorse, Jason walked back to the ship without saying a word, and on arriving relied on Argus to give the shipmates an account of the day's events. With the tests rigged and the Argonauts sure to lose, Mopsos asked Argus what they should do. Argus pointed out that he and his brothers were equally exposed to Aietes's wrath for having invited Jason to the palace. Argus went on to say that his mother, Chalkiope, had asked him to warn Jason of Aietes's deceit and suggested that he and his brothers join forces with the Argonauts to improve everyone's odds. Chalkiope further suggested that Argus should enlist the help of her sister, Medeia, who was popular with the common folk.

Jason readily agreed that four additional warriors would significantly boost his battle strength, especially since the brothers knew both the local terrain and the palace guards' fighting style. And while he was less certain about the value of

Chalkiope, he felt that any ally was preferable to an enemy. But what about Medeia, whose shiny, black hair, hazel-brown eyes, and sensuous lips had set his heart on fire? How could this exquisitely beautiful woman possibly help him and his men?

Argus's response was mysteriously opaque. He asserted that Medeia was more than she appeared to be, more powerful than a hundred warriors because of her knowledge of potions and drugs. Medeia alone, so Argus claimed, knew how to bend the odds of the test, but neither she nor his mother would risk taking sides unless the Argonauts made common cause with him and his brothers. Since an alliance made obvious sense, Jason asked his shipmates for an affirmative vote. Idas objected, arguing that Hellenic tradition was to fight and die like men without relying on witches and cowardly potions. Known for his quarrelsome nature, Idas averred that the highest virtues were honor and glory, not feminine ruses and lies.

But Jason stood tall in rebuttal. He pointed out that Aietes had started the chain of deceit; that what mattered was victory, not how it was gained; and that without the sisters' help they were bound to fail. With all others voicing agreement, Idas shut his mouth and acquiesced to the majority view. Jason gave Argus a big hug, formally sealing their alliance, and the crew exhaled a muted cheer. Shortly thereafter Argus left to inform his mother, and Jason ordered the crew to haul anchor and row the ship upriver, into view of the palace. All along the men had been ashamed of hiding like thieves in the reeds instead of strutting their prowess for all to see.

Later that day, sitting around the hearth nibbling bread and cheese, Jason was a bit flustered when he presented the story-game's most recent phase. At issue was his confidence in Medeia, whose potions and drugs were supposed to outwit King Aietes. When I suggested that the use of mysterious drugs was akin to the fantasies he had pledged to keep out of the game, Jason heatedly replied that he wasn't inventing miracles but needed help, and that Medeia was the best partner he could find. One young girl versus a king and his guards? Stuttering in search of the right word, Jason insisted Medeia was smart and inventive, and fully equipped to outwit Aietes's sclerotic mind. And this wasn't his opinion alone: Chariklo fully agreed that old Aietes was no match for young Medeia.

That said, Jason bid us good night and went to bed. Astounded and not a little surprised, I stared at Philyra and she stared back at me.

"Cheiron, unless I'm mistaken, this isn't the first time Jason has mentioned Chariklo in connection with the story-game. And his description of Medeia—shiny-black hair, hazel-brown eyes—perfectly matches Chariklo's looks. Whenever the boy refers to Medeia he seems to have Chariklo in mind. Is he confusing the two? Which of the two does he think he loves?"

"That depends which Jason you are talking about: the boy who lives on Pelion, or the Argonaut who presently camps out in Kolchis."

"The boy is real. The Argonaut is fiction."

"Yes, Philyra, though I'm not sure Jason would accept your distinction. The game requires him to think as if he were the other, feeling the other's experience as if it were his own. But if he feels the same as the other, which of the two is he? Since he can't be one *and* the other, it is natural for him to feel that he is both."

"Very nice, Cheiron, and so neatly analytical. But how does this two-in-one composite soul relate to Chariklo, your soon-to-be wife?"

"Oh Philyra, it's worse than you think. Jason told me in no uncertain terms that my role in the story-game is Aietes. So when his mind is in Kolchis, he hates me and loves Medeia. When he is here with us, spinning the story-game over supper, I am not sure what goes on in his mind."

When Argus entered his mother's chambers, he found her utterly distraught and lost in tears. Knowing how cruel Aietes could be, Chalkiope was deeply afraid for her sons. Something had to be done to save them, or they would be food for the fishes.

Trying to calm her fears, Argus told Chalkiope of Jason's agreement, which gave her a glimmer of hope where there had been darkness before. Yet Chalkiope also knew no matter how great the enthusiasm of her sons' well-intentioned young friends, evil Aietes could not be derailed by force alone. Evil had to be fought with evil! Aietes's murderous scheme had to be fought with Medeia's potions! Resolved to move from thought to action, Chalkiope rushed to her sister's apartment to win her support, only to find the usually stoic Medeia sobbing in boundless despair, convinced that Jason, the man of her dreams, would be killed by Aietes's fierce bulls.

What a strange pair of sisters. With Chalkiope determined to save her sons and Medeia desperate to keep Jason alive, the two couldn't have a more powerful argument for betraying their father and helping the Argonauts. But matters weren't as simple as that. What would happen to them, what would be their fate, after the Argonauts and the brothers had departed for Hellas? The obvious answer was that Chalkiope and Medeia would be at Aietes's mercy, of which he had none. Chalkiope knew well the penalty for treason and was prepared to make the ultimate sacrifice for her sons, but Medeia was young and ambitious, and not at all ready to die. She would support the Argonauts' cause only if her security was guaranteed and sworn to under oath by Jason himself. Although Chalkiope argued no one would ever learn of her role in sabotaging the tests, Medeia refused to budge, demanding to meet the Argonauts' leader at Hekate's temple early the next day.

When dawn spread over the distant horizon, Medeia commandeered her chariot and drove at full speed to the temple grove of Hekate, goddess of witchcraft and magic. Confessing her love for Jason to the divinity's three-headed likeness, Medeia prayed for a sign to help her choose between duty to country and desire for the blond-haired Hellenic prince. It was an impossible choice—a circle that couldn't be squared—but, swayed by sexual longing, Medeia persuaded herself that in the eyes of the goddess love was beyond good and evil. Indeed, at the very moment when Medeia imagined that the goddess would favor love above all else, bright sunshine flooded Hekate's dark temple. Where there had been doubt, there now was light, and, freed from qualms and scruples, Medeia stretched out on the dew-covered lawn, convinced her choice was the goddess's command.

Meanwhile, with Argus leading the way, Jason and Mopsos began their long walk to Hekate's shrine. Although anxious to meet Medeia again, Jason made Argus swear under oath that Medeia meant to seal the agreement, not deceive him or his men. Under the deal the Argonauts would protect the four brothers and, in return, Chalkiope and Medeia would divulge Aietes's plans. However, when Argus confessed not knowing why Medeia insisted on meeting at Hekate's shrine, Jason decided to bring along Mopsos, who was wise in the ways of prophecy.

Jason was in good spirits, confident in his abilities and

emboldened by Medeia's promised help. Nearing Hekate's precinct, Mopsos became aware of Jason's accelerating stride, unconsciously revealing his desire to be with Medeia. Mopsos correctly surmised what stirred Jason's heart and decided it would be best for Jason to meet the princess alone.

Advancing toward the temple, Jason espied a veiled figure at the sanctuary's gate. Uncertain of the person's identity, Jason slowed his pace when Medeia lifted her veil and revealed her radiant beauty to his amorous eyes. Unable to suppress her welling love, hazel-eyed Medeia confirmed her willingness to help, though if she did she would no longer be safe in Kolchis and would have to flee. Jason wanted the same thing—namely her and to escape from Kolchis. With amity and passion in perfect complement, Jason wrapped his arms around her waist, love travelling from soul to soul, man and woman feeling their hearts humming in tune. Momentarily lost to the world, only she and he seemed to exist, two being one, knowing without saying a word that they would quit Kolchis together and be happy forever. Love promised both what each desired: Medeia wanted Jason; Jason wanted Medeia and also her gold.

Jason spoke haltingly, though with considerable fervor—his face blushed, his breath shallow—about the lovers' hearts singing the same tune. Philyra looked visibly alarmed, wondering how Jason would know what falling in love was all about. Alas there was no time for questions or answers as Jason pushed the story-game forward to the upcoming tests that threatened the love that had scarcely begun. How could Jason possibly plow a four-acre field with untamed bulls and an unfamiliar tool? How could the Argonauts prevail over unknown numbers of iron-armed Kolchian guards?

Deeply happy only a moment ago, Jason bemoaned his lopsided odds. He had no future; his prospect was death. Not so Medeia! Aware that their prospects were bleak, the princess was determined to even the odds. Pushing aside all thoughts of love, Medeia drew up a plan that combined courage with ruse in order to thwart Aietes's evil intent. Eager to impress the man she loved, Medeia coolly explained her strategy.

While admitting that the plowing test posed multiple dangers, Medeia asserted that success was at hand if the bulls could be made to pull forward without attacking the driver. If the bulls were to act like dull oxen, Jason could devote all his attention to handling the heavy moldboard plow. All he had to do was hold the plow's handle in his left hand and the goad in his right, and steer the plow straight ahead. Making turns and reversing direction would be more difficult, but not impossible as long as Jason remembered to swing the plow extra wide at each turn. To make it all work, Medeia would give the animals a rare potion, converting their bullness to oxlike docility.

The second test, the hand-to-hand battle against the king's guards, was an altogether different matter. Medeia assumed Aietes would line up two contingents against the Argonauts— one Hittite, the other Thrakian—outnumbering the Hellenes by at least two to one. Moreover, the palace guards would be equipped with iron spears and iron swords, giving them a distinct advantage over the bronze-armed Argonauts. Medeia saw only one way of leveling the battlefield, and that was using a dirty trick. Fearing Jason might reject her plan as unmanly or shameful, she refused to disclose what she had in mind. But when Jason pushed for an answer, Medeia said she would add a special oil and some herbs to the soldiers' beer.

Jason was baffled. Pour oil into beer? Yes, Medeia explained, white hellebore mixed with oil would purge the guards' bowels.

Her only concern was timing, namely how to make the guards soil themselves at the exact time when they lined up to battle the Argonauts. Visualizing a whole army browning their tunics made Jason laugh. Surely Medeia was making a joke. But the princess was deadly serious, saying this was her one and only plan. Annoyed by Jason's reaction, and possibly embarrassed by plotting to have grown men lose control of their bowels, Medeia left abruptly without saying goodbye, anxious to get back to the palace before she was missed.

When Jason told Mopsos what Medeia had in mind, Mopsos was outright dismissive, doubting Medeia could do what she promised. Argus, however, strongly defended his aunt's capabilities and extolled her knowledge of tonics and drugs. If Medeia said she would tranquilize the bulls and fece-size the soldiers, then that was precisely what she would do, no doubt about it. Jason very much wanted to believe that Medeia could do what she said she could, if only because neither he nor Mopsos had any alternative plan. As Jason saw it, the Argonauts either relied on Medeia or faced impossible odds, which meant they had no choice at all. But while Jason was ready to put his fate in Medeia's hands, his shipmates were far from persuaded to do the same.

Back at the ship, Jason led the debate about Medeia's plan. The argument was noisy and long, but since no one could think of anything better, the Argonauts bowed to necessity and accepted Medeia's ideas. However, not to be completely outdone, the men added three measures of their own. Echion demanded that a four-legged beast be sacrificed to placate the gods and Euphemos be instructed to rustle an unlucky sheep. Erginos asked Mopsos to analyze the flight of hawks to predict the outcome of the forthcoming tests. And Peleus, more practical and rational than the rest, urged the crew to practice and rehearse: Jason learning how to use the plow, and the men learning how to fight in group formation. Peleus made sense. Argus went off to find an old plow for Jason to practice with while Peleus explained in detail how fighting as a unit was more effective than battling one guardsman at a time.

Meleager and Leodokos, renowned individual champions, objected to fighting as a team, but when Peleus demonstrated his novel formation, the men practiced the rest of the day, lining up shoulder to shoulder, interlocking their shields, and thrusting their spears toward the enemy like a hedgehog his spines. As Jason got used to the heavy Kolchian plow and the men learned to fight in phalanx, the Argonauts' confidence grew by leaps, although everyone was also fully aware that without Medeia's intervention their training might well be for naught.

The palace was equally preoccupied with the upcoming tests. Medeia paced nervously back and forth in her suite. Had her promise to Jason been overly rash? Was it wise to deceive her father? Did she really love Jason or was it mere passion? And how could she tell one from the other?

Chalkiope was similarly upset. Her sons had deserted the king, and though her sister had promised to help, Chalkiope knew Medeia was fickle and prone to changing her mind. Then there was the king. Aietes told everyone who was willing to listen that the tests were an easy win, but the more he boasted and bragged, the less confident he appeared about facing thirty-four warriors whose skills and tactics he didn't know. Queen Eidyia promptly apprised Perses, her lover, of the king's ebbing confidence about the tests. Perses, in turn, assured Eidyia that all was under control, then alerted Apsyrtos that the time may have come to overthrow the king. Apsyrtos pledged his support, figuring if Perses killed Aietes the people would tear the usurper to pieces and give the crown to him as the legitimate heir.

At daybreak the two camps stirred to life. The Argonauts rowed their ship to the Plain of Ares, where the contests would take place. Aietes, resplendent in shining armor and golden helmet, impatiently waited for Jason to arrive. Jason slung his sword over his shoulder, fit his left arm to his bronze-plated shield, and held his ashen spear firmly in his right hand. Thus armed, Jason stepped forward using his shield to ward off the charging bulls, a tactic that slowly tired them out. Seizing one of the beasts by its horns, Jason kicked its front leg and forced it onto its knees. Repeating the same trick with the other bull, he placed the yoke around the beasts' necks and fastened the plow's pole to the yoke.

Ready and set to plow, Jason pricked the bulls with his goad, urging them on. This was the critical moment: would the bulls obey Jason's command or turn around their horns, intent on goring him? To everyone's surprise the bulls obediently pulled forward, Medeia's potion having tamed their temper without reducing their strength. Once into the plowing rhythm, Jason worked furrow after furrow at a steady pace and finished the four-acre field by mid-afternoon. With the first test completed, he walked back to the ship to quench his thirst and rally his shipmates for the second round.

Aietes was furious. What had happened to his bulls? They had always killed the plowman and never pulled the plow! But never mind: he was certain his palace guards would soon separate the Argonauts from life. Aietes fielded one hundred guards, equally split between Thrakians and Hittites, against Jason's motley thirty-four men. When Jason protested about

Aietes's fielding three times the number of his warriors, the king mockingly retorted that since the Hellenes were descended from gods, they should have no trouble fighting more than one opponent at the same time.

Expecting as much from Aietes, the Argonauts promptly formed their two-rank phalanx, with Jason gallantly taking the rightmost position. Their solid wall of interlocking shields and leveled spears caught the Kolchian mercenaries by surprise. Clueless as to how to engage a phalanx, the Kolchian advance came to a halt. Aietes jumped to his feet, calling his guards cowards and worse, and commanded Apsyrtos to drive them forward using the whip. But as the Kolchians regrouped, their tunics suddenly turned brown: a telltale sign of battle fright. When the Kolchian rear started to laugh, calling the frontline cowardly chickens, the afflicted guards forgot about the Hellenes and turned on their mocking comrades, whose tunics were getting equally soiled. Soon all one hundred of Aietes's guards, embarrassed by their sphincters' malfunctions, were battling each other in a vain attempt to save face.

The Argonauts watched in amazement as the palace guards methodically destructed themselves: Hittites killing red-haired Thrakians, and Thrakians felling bearded Hittites in rapid succession. The suicidal craze lasted barely fifteen minutes in all. Spearheads crushed breastplates, swords severed heads from bodies, and man after man ate the dust of the plain. When the massacre was over, one hundred of the king's guards lay dead without the Argonauts having raised a single hand. With his court watching in stunned silence, Aietes was deeply humiliated, and he wondered how his carefully made plan had so utterly failed. Neither the bulls' docile demeanor nor the guards' soiling their tunics seemed random events. Two or three soldiers might get sick, but not every single one, and not at exactly the same time. Without knowing who did what and how it was done, Aietes was convinced a member of his court had betrayed him, hoping to benefit from his humiliation.

By the time Aietes returned to the royal palace, the throne room was filled with family members, nobles, officers, and staff, all eager to discuss what happened and hear what the king had to say. Aietes was furious and instantly harangued his audience, accusing sundry and all of disloyalty and treason, promising to prosecute ruthlessly whoever had sabotaged the tests. Aietes's anger was frightening to watch, yet more frightening still was what everyone knew he was going to do. Everyone would be suspect, everyone would be interrogated, and no one would be safe, whether guilty or not.

Aietes eyed his brother Perses with withering contempt; glared at Chalkiope, whose sons had deserted him; chided Apsyrtos for the guards' self-destruction; and cast a pensively suspicious look at Medeia, whose medicinal expertise made her the most likely betrayer. Sensing Aietes's growing suspicion, Medeia took fright, her legs getting wobbly and weak. She had to get out before it was too late and, wasting no time, resolutely wrapped a veil over her head and headed straight for the Argonauts' ship.

Perses felt equally at risk. The king had never trusted him because he was next in line to the throne. No matter how scrupulously loyal, no matter how devoutly obedient he had been, Aietes had always hated his guts, repeatedly sending him on dangerous missions, hoping he would be captured or killed. Now, after years of studied subordination, Perses was no longer willing to live under Aietes's despotic thumb. Enough was enough! Knowing Queen Eidyia, his secret paramour, would share his decision and that Apsyrtos would follow his lead, Perses resolved to challenge Aietes in open court. Since no one had questioned the king before, the throne room fell quiet when Perses stood and accused Aietes of mishandling the Argonaut landing. Question after question poured from Perses' mouth: Why hadn't the Argonauts been killed on arrival? What was the purpose of staging these ridiculous tests? Who would pay for the dead: the king or the treasury? And who would protect the state's gold with most of the palace guards dead?

Aietes couldn't believe his ears. This was open rebellion—Perses was after his throne. He had to arrest the bastard and tear out his traitorous tongue. Yet when Aietes's henchmen came to put Perses in chains, Apsyrtos stood by his side, and neither party was willing to yield an inch. The confrontation was at a tipping point. Weapons were drawn, and a hasty move by either side could have turned the room into a killing field.

Yet the assembled audience, having seen enough bloodshed for one day, urged everyone to drop their arms, with the result that no one threw a first punch, raised a sword, or talked trash, least of all Apsyrtos, who wanted to be seen as preserving the peace. Perses too was happy to avoid a bloody melee. Throwing down the gauntlet had gained him public support. Now it was merely a matter of awaiting the right time to kill Aietes and assume his throne.

Jason had been talking nonstop, with an occasional facial spasm reminding us of his long-cured disease. Even Nessos, who was usually a skeptical fox, hung on Jason's every word and pressed him to reveal his plan for ending the game. Would Aietes die? Who would kill him? Would Perses kill Apsyrtos or the other way around? When Jason said he didn't yet know, Nessos kept pushing him to reveal how the story would end.

"Nessos, I honestly don't know. Aietes's time is up. Someone will kill him, I am sure of that—Perses, Apsyrtos, or Jason, but surely not Medeia."

"Jason, how do you know what Medeia might do?"

"I asked Chariklo how she would act if she were Medeia, but her answer didn't make sense."

"Hey! We are talking about Medeia, not Chariklo. Or am I confused?"

"Not really. For the story-game to be realistic, I have to think in terms of actual people. How else would I know what a woman feels or how a king thinks?"

"But Chariklo is not Medeia, and Cheiron isn't a king. He is your father."

"No, you're wrong. Cheiron is not my father! Cheiron is short and dark-skinned, and has a black beard like all Pelion men. I am already taller than he and have blue eyes and blond hair. I am not his son!"

When Nessos came running to tell me what Jason had said, I realized that I should have told Jason the truth a long time ago. So I took my son by the hand, walked outside, and told him how I had found him thirteen years ago on the shore of Pagasae Bay. I fibbed that I didn't know who his biological parents were, but asserted that he has been my son since I adopted him when he was three weeks old. I also told him that I had loved him from the moment I had found him, and would love him to the end of my days.

Jason listened quietly to my account but kept asking who his real parents might be. So I repeated what I had told Philyra and Nessos and everyone else on Pelion many times before, which was that I didn't know. Yes, I lied, but for good reason. I had promised Jason's parents never to reveal the boy's identity, and I never would, not in order to get those ten sheep every year, but because no good would be served if the truth were known. King Peleas was still alive and as paranoid as ever. If Jason had gone off in search of his parents, he would have endangered not only himself but also all of us on Pelion. So I stuck to my story. Jason moped about the rest of the day, not knowing how to think of himself or who he was from one hour to the next. We talked back and forth for a long time, but by the end of the day he seemed to accept his identity.

"Cheiron, I am sadly confused. I know you are my father and you love me while the other one doesn't even know I exist. Could we forget my rude behavior and go back to where we were before?"

"Jason, of course!"

"Thanks. I feel so much better. Since we're talking, I might as well ask you how I can bring the story-game to a plausible end. For reasons I don't understand, I am stuck—unable to move the story forward a single hour, not to mention another day."

"Jason, you've been playing the game exceedingly well, but may have overlooked a subtle shift in your narrative. The early part of the story, the voyage from Iolkos to Kolchis, was relatively easy. Sailing all the way to Kolchis had a momentum all its own. The weather changed every which way, and you came across all kinds of folks, while Kolchis was always the ultimate goal. However, once you reached Kolchis, the story-game changed. Instead of dealing with weather and geography, you now had to deal with people, what to say, and how to act in order to achieve your objective. And that was where you made a mistake. Rather than invent the people of Kolchis the way you invented Hypsipyle, Kyzikos, and Phineus, you began to model some characters on persons you know. For example you cast me in the role of Aietes to give your story a sheen of reality, but it confused not only the game but also you."

"Cheiron, you are so right! I am stuck because you are Aietes. He is bad, and his rule must end, but how can I kill him when he is you? If you were to stop being him, I could kill the bastard without guilt."

Needless to say I was happy to quit playing Aietes, a character with whom I had nothing in common. And I was doubly happy about being out of the story-game: no longer a participant, but merely the game's coach. Unfortunately I couldn't have been any more wrong, as I was soon to find out.

With the air cleared of parenthood issues and such, Jason picked up the story where he had left off. Medeia left the king's meeting and drove her chariot at full speed to Argo's anchorage. Hearing her desperate calls, Jason ferried across the river and brought Medeia on board. The princess was frightened to death, certain that Aietes would arrest her, try her for treason, and hand her the hemlock cup. She pleaded with Jason to cut the ship's hawsers and row downriver before Aietes could block the port.

Jason, anxious to please Medeia and bound by oath to protect her, immediately ordered the crew to ready their oars and cast off, but to Jason's surprise none of the Argonauts obeyed his command. The shipmates resolutely refused to leave Kolchis just yet. The men had rowed to Kolchis in search of gold, not for Medeia, and while Jason was befuddled by love, they were not. Leodokos spoke first, followed by Periklymenos and Erginos. All argued that the perfect time to seize the state treasury was when the Kolchians were fighting each other—their civil war was a Zeus-given opportunity to grab what they had come for. Peleus suggested that twenty of the shipmates advance to the treasury compound and overpower the guards while the rest of the crew stayed behind to protect the ship.

Medeia listened to the men's deliberation with growing concern, fearing that instead of leaving Kolchis posthaste she would be compelled to betray her country again. The ship Argo was her only means of escape, and the only way to be taken aboard was to help the Argonauts steal her people's gold. What should she do? Well, with a hundred palace guards lying dead on the Plain of Ares, Medeia figured that no more than ten would be protecting the treasury that night, a fact that favored the Argonauts' plan. So, treason being like sticky glue that never lets go, Medeia offered to guide the Argonauts to the treasury, proving to Jason that he and she were a team. Jason was overjoyed and immediately organized the raiding patrol. Then, with Medeia at his side, he led his twenty-men-strong contingent on the long march to the treasury site.

Meanwhile things went from bad to worse at the palace. When Apsyrtos stopped the king and the king's brother from fighting it out in public, everyone fled, fearing what had barely been avoided. The Kolchian nobles were deeply upset by the rivalry within the royal clan and urged Perses to apologize to King Aietes, his brother. Perses shrewdly agreed on the condition that the king guaranteed his personal security. With Queen Eidyia acting as intermediary, a meeting was arranged between the two brothers, but while Aietes was willing to make peace, Perses was not. Faking a brotherly embrace, Perses thrust his dagger into Aietes's left side, severing the abdominal aorta and causing the king's instant death. His tunic splattered with blood, Perses claimed he had acted in self-defense, that he had been merely standing his ground. Although many suspected that Perses was lying, Apsyrtos confirmed his account and thereby assured his uncle's succession to the throne.

Unaware of the events at the palace, Jason's raiders marched at double pace to the Kolchian treasury. Since their window of opportunity was narrow, the men planned to rely on ruse and execute the raid with dispatch. Medeia walked ahead and falsely informed the guards that King Aietes, her father, had agreed to pay the Hellenic invaders one hundred gold talents provided they left Kolchis at sunrise. Her order was to admit the Argonauts into the compound and hand them the gold. The guards were baffled six ways to one, but Medeia was the king's daughter, and no one dared to challenge her. So the guards, the foolish souls, opened the gate. Jason promptly disarmed them and put them in shackles—a fate they justly deserved.

The treasury compound was a sight to behold. On the left was a vault holding gold bars and nuggets; on the right were wooden racks stacked with gold-speckled fleeces, and the compound's center accommodated two longish structures for the guards and the treasury staff. The men made a beeline for the vault, eager to carry off as much gold as they could. But when they found the door locked and asked the captured guards for the key, the guards confessed that only Aietes and Apsyrtos could access the vault. Jason was stunned. After months of braving rough seas and pounding storms, no door would stand in his way. He summoned Areius and Talaos, his two strongest mates, and ordered them to fashion a battering ram.

The pair repeatedly rammed the vault's iron door, but to no avail. When Talaos tired, Meleagros grabbed the ram, then Erytion gave it a try, and eventually every member of the raiding party took a crack at breaking the door. But the vault held firm. No one kept track of the time as minutes stretched into an hour and longer. The original plan of grabbing the gold with lightning speed had utterly failed, and the noise of the battering ram alerted all of Kolchis that the country's treasury was under siege.

The Kolchian response was quick. Apsyrtos rushed to the treasury with his remaining guards, shut the unguarded gate, and demanded that the Argonauts surrender. However, peeking over the wall, Jason realized that Apsyrtos had fewer than thirty men—hardly an overwhelming force. So Jason rejected Apsyrtos's demand, asking instead for free passage and as much gold as he could carry in exchange for the imprisoned guards.

Apsyrtos laughed at the bluff, then coldly replied that Jason had two choices: deal with him and go free, or wait for the army under Perses and be tortured and killed.

Listening from behind the wall, Medeia heard Apsyrtos refer to Perses as the leader of the army. Perses, not Aietes? The gold hoard had been Aietes's foremost concern for a very long time, so why didn't he come himself? Sinister thoughts entered Medeia's mind; she wondered what had happened after she had escaped from the palace. Did Aietes suspect her of rigging the tests, or had Perses accused her of poisoning the guards? Having no answers, she called out to Apsyrtos, asking him where Aietes was. Hearing his sister's voice, Apsyrtos realized that Medeia was with Jason but didn't yet know that Aietes was dead.

Faking joy over hearing her voice, Apsyrtos requested to speak to Medeia in private, hoping sweet talk could persuade his sister to take his side against Perses. Jason's first thought was to decline Apsyrtos's request, but he eventually acceded to Medeia's entreaties, provided the two would meet inside the compound's walls. Guaranteed safe conduct, Apsyrtos entered the site, led Medeia aside, and told her that Perses had killed their father. He furthermore confessed that he needed Medeia's help to protect Eidyia and Chalkiope and avenge Aietes's death. Apsyrtos, of course, was twisting the truth. While Perses had killed Aietes, Apsyrtos had condoned the dastardly deed, and Eidyia planned to marry Perses and was in no danger at all. Apsyrtos merely wanted Medeia's endorsement to strengthen his popular support and thereby secure his dynastic position.

Medeia, however, wasn't thinking about power and regnancy. She was gripped by contrition and bitter remorse, blaming herself for her father's death. Whatever Aietes had been, he was her father and her king, and now he was dead because of her—because her heart had succumbed to Jason's charm. If only everything could be the way it had been. Sobbing uncontrollably, Medeia rested her head on the chest of Apsyrtos, who consolingly embraced her trembling frame.

Jason, standing out of earshot, watched Apsyrtos with growing disquiet, seeing not what transpired but what his jealous mind conjured. Medeia was crying, wasn't she? And Apsyrtos was constraining her, was he not? While the night was black and visibility was poor, Jason trusted his eyes, and his eyes called for action. So he raised his weapon and, aiming with care, buried his spear deep between Apsyrtos's shoulder blades, piercing his princely heart. Apsyrtos exhaled a pitiful moan as blood gushed from his mouth. He was dead as his body hit the ground.

Medeia was stupefied: her brother dead by Jason's hand? But why? This didn't make sense. The world had gone mad. She had to recover reality or go insane. Loathing the present and longing for the unrecoverable past, Medeia matured from maiden to woman in one lightning moment. When Jason tried to comfort her, she looked at him as if she had never seen him before.

It goes without saying that Philyra was deeply upset when told that Jason had killed another man. Didn't he feel regret, and hadn't he learned from the death of Kyzikos? What was the point of the story-game if it didn't foster Jason's conscience, if it failed to make him a better man? And hadn't Jason granted Apsyrtos safe passage? Whether in play or in life, a man's word must be sacred, and Philyra wasted no time taking Jason to task.

"Jason, why did your Jason murder Medeia's brother? He came to talk, not to hurt you."

"Philyra, don't you see? Apsyrtos was bad. He conspired with Perses to kill his own father."

"But the story-game Jason didn't know that. Only you knew he was bad because you said so in an earlier part of the story. And Medeia didn't know either. How are you going to explain this mess to her?"

"Medeia loves me and will understand. Perhaps I acted too hastily, but my intention was pure."

"No, Jason, you are wrong on two counts: you acted impulsively, and your impulse was triggered by jealousy, which is the opposite of goodness and decency. Medeia will not forgive you."

"I will let Chariklo be the judge."

There it was again: Jason confusing and fusing Chariklo

with Medeia in his ever more twisted mind. Philyra accused Jason acting out of jealousy, which didn't make sense since Medeia was talking to her brother, not to a possible lover. And why did he ask Chariklo about Apsyrtos's death? Chariklo had no brother and couldn't truly empathize with Medeia. Apsyrtos's death was merely an error that Jason refused to retract because he believed that changing a past event would destroy the story-game's apparent reality and make it into a fictional tale.

Nessos averred that I was wrong and Philyra was right. When Jason saw Apsyrtos embrace Medeia, he saw Chariklo in Apsyrtos's arms, not Medeia. Jason was jealous, and he hurled his spear. Nessos believed that Jason was walking two separate tracks, one in the real world, the other in his mind. Jason's *dim-ma* perceived both as real, although one could be seen and touched while the other was a progression from memory. Nessos said Jason had trouble using both tracks at the same time because every so often they crossed in his mind. What crossed in his mind? What was Nessos talking about? Nessos eyed me with pity: didn't I see what was happening? Medeia and Chariklo had become one and the same in Jason's mind.

But the two weren't the same. Chariklo and I would marry in less than a month, and the story-game would come to an end. Chariklo would live with me while Jason could have his Medeia all to himself. But perhaps Nessos was right when he talked about crisscrosses in Jason's head, thoughts intended for one place ending up in another. Jason had quoted Chariklo more than once to explain Medeia's feelings and moods. And he got Medeia's words from talking to Chariklo for hours on end. Only yesterday the two sat under the oak tree all afternoon. Who sought out whom and why? It was time I talked to my fiancée.

"Chariklo, darling, you look more beautiful every day. I bet you had a good night's sleep!"

"Sleep is dreaming, sunlight, and flowers, love and desire. But no, I slept hardly at all."

"Perhaps you are anxious about the wedding, our future life?"

"No. I can hardly wait. My worry is Jason. I'm going to be his mom, but he thinks I'm something else."

"Philyra is his mom. You'll be his aunt."

"His aunt? Don't be ridiculous: I'm only five years older than he."

"So be his best friend."

"Cheiron, listen, being best friends is the problem. When he talks of Medeia, he holds my hand and strokes my hair. What should I do?"

"Talk about our wedding and tell him to keep his hands to himself."

So there it was: the story-game had come full circle, biting its own tail. It had begun with Jason playing a game, and now the game was playing with Jason. How will he react when Chariklo, no matter how gently, explains to him that the love of lovers is different from the love between sister and brother? Will he blame Medeia for Chariklo's rebuff? Will he change the course of the game?

Philyra believed Medeia would be deeply upset over the death of Apsyrtos, and so she was. When Medeia saw her brother's corpse lying crumpled on the ground, she could neither deny what had happened nor fully accept that it had. Her father was dead, and now also her brother. Were their deaths her fault? Had they died because she had tamed the bulls and poisoned the guards? Too numb to form a coherent thought, Medeia cried softly into the night, rocking from side to side. Apsyrtos was dead, and Jason had killed him, but what about her? And who was Jason, and why was he here?

Jason was equally confused, though mostly about himself. He had hurled his spear to protect his beloved and killed who he thought had attacked her, but now learned with dismay that Medeia mourned her brother and blamed Jason for his death. Worst of all Medeia spoke not a word, demanded no answer, and acted as if she had never seen him before. An hour ago they had laughed and babbled; now all was silence, their souls wide apart.

As Medeia knelt at Apsyrtos's body and Jason stood aside, each passing second more painful than the one before, loud voices came from across the compound's wall. It was Perses shouting for Apsyrtos. When Medeia heard his voice, she knew she had to think quickly or lose her head to Perses's sword. Telling Jason to hold his tongue, she called back to Perses, saying the Argonauts had captured Apsyrtos, and asked what he wanted from him.

Now it was Perses's turn to be surprised: Apsyrtos was the Hellenes's prisoner, and Medeia was inside the walls! Had she joined the Hellenes, as Aietes had suspected, or was she a prisoner too? For his kingship to be secure, Perses knew that he needed a royal sponsor—either Medeia because she was popular with the people, or Apsyrtos because he commanded the palace guard. Comparing the two, Medeia seemed the safer bet because she was less of a threat. Having made his decision, Perses wasted no time and asked to speak to Medeia alone.

Medeia suggested they talk across the wall, and Perses agreed. She explained that the Hellenes had captured her when she had run away from the palace, but that they promised to release her unharmed if she gave them gold. When Apsyrtos had arrived with his handful of guards, he had walked into a trap and was captured by the Hellenes. Medeia said she wanted to go home to her mother and sister, rid the country of the Hellenic intruders, and return Kolchis to peace and prosperity.

Picking up on Medeia's pitch, Perses proclaimed that his goals for Kolchis were exactly the same, but that he could not do it alone. Would Medeia join his court for the greater good of the Kolchian nation?

Medeia's answer was a bitter laugh. As a prisoner of the Hellenes, who surely would kill her, she couldn't help anyone, least of all herself. But Perses was confident of striking a bargain with Jason—something like her freedom for his—and possibly achieving other objectives as well. So Medeia went to fetch Jason, warning him again not to reveal that Apsyrtos was dead.

Jason was determined to stand his ground, showing neither worry nor fear on meeting the new king. So he shaved his upper lip and combed his hair and beard, slipped on his toe-bending sandals, and strapped leather greaves to his shins. Putting on a newly washed tunic and draping a purple cloak across his shoulders, Jason placed his boar-tusk helmet on his head and used his belt to hold his sword. He looked as splendid as any Hellenic prince before and since. Facing Perses across the wall, Jason continued his charade by staying mute, purposely waiting for Perses to speak first.

Perses averred what Jason already knew: the treasury compound was surrounded by two hundred Kolchian soldiers; the Argonauts couldn't escape; their only option was to surrender. Two hundred warriors were more than Jason had expected, but whether there were one hundred or two hundred the Argonauts were badly outnumbered either way. Yet

Jason didn't flinch. He straightforwardly advised Perses that if attacked, he would kill Apsyrtos, Medeia, and the captured guards and then fight to the death, taking down as many Kolchian soldiers as he could.

Impressed by Jason's bravura, Perses said Jason got it all wrong. There was no gain in more bloodshed, and Jason and his men were free to withdraw provided they released Medeia and the guards, returned to their ship, and left Kolchis without delay. Jason was dumbstruck, unsure how to reply. He happily would have traded the guards for free passage, but Medeia was his, and why didn't Perses demand that Apsyrtos be freed? Not knowing what Perses had in mind, Jason took a calculated chance, saying his men had come to Kolchis for gold and were unwilling to leave with empty hands. But if Perses would pay a ransom for Apsyrtos, a deal could be made.

Perses, of course, had no interest in freeing Apsyrtos. He wanted no rival to his rule, but after killing Aietes, the father, he couldn't very well kill the son too. So he slyly suggested that Jason could have the gold he wanted if, somehow, Apsyrtos were not part of the prisoner exchange. Jason couldn't believe his luck: he had feared that Perses would seek revenge for Apsyrtos's death, but having killed Apsyrtos now gave him a bargaining chip. Even Medeia would have to accept that Apsyrtos was doomed either way: what happened was history and couldn't be changed.

After a deliberative pause, Jason accepted Perses's offer on the assumption that the Argonauts would be allowed to enter the vault. Perses, however, kept the vault tightly locked, and, grinning from ear to ear, gave Jason one of the gold-speckled fleeces instead.

Later that day, when Jason reported the game's latest phase, Philyra was pleased that Jason and Perses had made a deal instead of fighting it out. Although the game wasn't finished, Jason signaled that, except for unforeseen snags, the rest of the story would be routine. The Argonauts would take the fleece, set their prisoners free, hand over Apsyrtos's corpse, and sail back to Hellas with Medeia on board.

But hadn't Perses asked Medeia to join his court and govern Kolchis with him? Yes, but Medeia was free to do as she pleased, and, being in love with Jason, would come home with him. And so, after playing the story-game for more than a year, it had reached its happy end. There was much clapping of hands all around, everyone congratulating Jason for a job well done and everyone fully aware that the voyage wasn't merely a story but an experience lived in the mind. When no more praise could be added, when the game had been lauded five ways to none, the conversation gradually shifted back to everyday life on Pelion.

The day's topic was our wedding: Cheiron and Chariklo would finally tie the knot. The ceremony was scheduled for the following week. Everyone living on the mountain would attend. We would eat spit-roasted boar and bowls of gruel, and wash it all down with gallons of beer. The ceremony would take place when the sun was at its zenith, and everyone would have a really good time. Philyra and Chariklo were planning each step of the feast—who would do what and who would sit where and who would conduct the marriage oath.

With the wedding only days away, Chariklo's exuberance grew by the minute, her eyes beacons of happiness and her voice bubbling with joy. Jason got tired and went to bed, but this was Chariklo's moment, and she made it last well into the night.

The next morning Nessos took me aside, saying how happy Chariklo looked and how pleased he was that our wedding was finally on. He also thought the story-game had been a great success, teaching Jason many things and maturing him well beyond his years. Yet with everything going so well, he had one worry left: the spirals in Jason's blood. Now that the story-game was done, Nessos suggested we test Jason's blood again to make sure that the spirals were gone.

Although I hadn't noticed any facial tics or other spasms bothering Jason in quite some time, Nessos's advice made sense, and I set out to explain to Jason what we intended to do. But Jason was nowhere to be found—not then, not the next day, and not the day after. When Philyra noticed his clothes were gone too, our worry turned into serious angst. Where was he, and why had he left without saying a word?

Imagine my surprise when, three days after Jason's disappearance, Pholos wandered into the cave and calmly informed me that Jason was staying with him. Jason had told Pholos that because of the wedding there was too much commotion at the cave for him to wrap up the story-game. Not wanting to get into an argument with silly-ass Pholos, I simply thanked him for his kindness, told him about the blood test Nessos wanted to do, and extracted from him a promise that he would bring Jason to the wedding whether Jason liked it or not.

Nessos went up to Pholos's hut the very next day, pricked Jason's finger, and got his sample of *dara*. Using the same curved glasses we had used five years ago, we found not a single wiggly spiral in Jason's blood. Jason was cured; the disease was gone. Philyra was so happy she cried for an hour after hearing the news.

On the fifth day after Jason had moved out, I too made my way to Pholos's abode, hoping to learn what was troubling my son. Seeing me ambling up the path, Jason ran down to meet me, and gave me a big hug and kisses on both cheeks. Yes, he said, he was fine. Completing the story-game had turned out to be harder than he had expected. He needed time to reflect, to sort out his thoughts, and he was thankful to Pholos for not asking him to explain himself. But no, he wasn't ready to come home, not yet. The voyage had proven to be unbelievably strenuous, physically and mentally. Rowing the ship for months on end, confronting all sorts of contingencies, and dealing with Aietes and his family was bitterly exhausting. Jason simply needed a rest.

"Jason, I quite understand. You need a vacation, and so does your mind. But you said that you completed the game. Is the ship back in Hellas?"

"Cheiron, of course not. That would be totally unrealistic. Sailing back from Kolchis will take as many days as it took to get there. It will be months before Argo will reenter Pagasae Bay, assuming the crew will take the gold-flecked fleece to Iolkos rather than to Korinthos or some other place."

"Wouldn't that prolong the voyage, require more rowing, and cause more pain?"

"Yes, but Korinthos is the richest city in Hellas and presumably would pay most for the gold."

"I see what you mean. But say, what happened when you left Kolchis? Did Perses stick to the deal, and did everyone make it back to the ship?"

"Perses got what he wanted: Apsyrtos's death left him without a rival, and Medeia's joining his court assured him of the people's support."

"Medeia joined Perses's court? I don't understand."

"Well, neither did I—certainly not at the time, and frankly it still doesn't make sense. But the fact is that Medeia chose to remain in Kolchis, which left me no choice but to sail off alone."

"Was Jason caught off guard?"

"I was, but I shouldn't have been. I am a Hellene while Medeia is a Kolchian princess. We come from different lands, mine at the center and hers at the edge of the world. What is normal to one is foreign to the other. Then there was the death of Apsyrtos. Medeia didn't like him, but he was her brother, and when I wounded him, she called me a killer. Her father too was a nasty old man, but, as she said, he was her father, and she owed him her fealty."

"But Perses killed her father. Wasn't that a perfect reason to leave?"

"Her father's murder has to be avenged, and, with Apsyrtos dead, it is her duty to see justice done. If she had left, Perses would be king forever."

"And what about Jason? What are his plans?"

"I honestly don't know. Sailing to Kolchis was great. No other life will even come close."

EPILOGOS

The Argonauts spent a year and a half making the voyage out, lost five shipmates on the way, and, for all their troubles, came back with a single gold-laced fleece. Most bitter of all, Jason fell in love, but his love was unrequited, leaving him with a broken heart.

When Jason came to my wedding and congratulated Chariklo and me, his eyes didn't sparkle; his gaiety was fake. He never returned to the cave, preferring to live with Pholos instead. Over the next several years, Jason visited Philyra now and then but seemed anxious to avoid me. The few times our paths crossed, he was uneasy—not showing any hostility, but eager to get away. Then, on a beautiful morning in early May, he came to the cave to say goodbye. He was nineteen years old, healthy and strong, a fully grown man determined to make his way in the world. There were tears all around, hugs and kisses, and then he was gone. None of us ever saw him again.

As the years went by, Pelion's isolation gradually eased; our people mixed more freely with the Minyans in Iolkos and to the south. My growing reputation as a teacher and healer encouraged more parents to enroll their sons in my school, most notably the great Peleus, who entrusted his son Achilles to my care. Those were good years—at least they seemed to be good—and every so often we heard bits of news about Jason that seemed equally good. One rumor was that he had settled in Korinthos and married a local beauty named Glauke, fathered two children, and made a fortune in commerce. But there were other stories as well, claiming that Jason had sailed a ship to Kolchis, married a beautiful foreign princess, and brought back a gold-flecked fleece, which they now called *the* Golden Fleece. Jason was said to have made that voyage ten years ago, which was completely impossible because ten years ago Jason was sixteen and lived with Pholos on Pelion. Not knowing what to make of these rumors, I decided to pay Pholos a visit and hear what he had to say.

Never my favorite person, Pholos offered me a cup of stale beer and a wedge of old cheese when I came to his hut. It was six years since Jason had suddenly left without any warning, and Pholos said he missed him every day. He remembered Jason as inquisitive and questioning, not unpleasantly so, but straight-out obsessive about anything having to do with the Hellenes and their way of life. Jason was convinced that he was of Hellenic blood and wanted to know what the Hellenes were like—how they talked and thought, and how they were different from us. Pholos thought at first that Jason's interest in all things Hellenic was a passing fancy, but when the boy dug into the minutest details of Hellenic culture and mimicked Hellenic habits and speech, Pholos came to accept the fact that Jason wanted to emulate our oppressors' culture. Pholos initially was unsure how to proceed, but after Jason told him that he planned to live in Hellas when he was grown up, Pholos taught him the Hellenic way of life as best as he could.

Apart from his Hellenic fixation, Jason was thoroughly

pleasant company. He was even-tempered, rarely angry or upset, sparing of words, and perhaps a bit sad. Sometimes he talked of Philyra, though never, not once in six years of living with Pholos, did he mention Chariklo or me. The one subject Jason never tired of talking about was the story-game of sailing to Kolchis. He told the story, or parts of it, countless times, each retelling an elaboration of what he had told before. Pholos, closing his eyes as if in pain, confessed that he often worried about the boy's senses, since Jason typically referred to the voyage as if it had actually taken place. On one occasion when Pholos tried to tell Jason that the voyage was only a story and not something that had actually happened, Jason got furious, ran up to the peak, and stayed away for more than a week. Jason eventually came back, but only after Pholos promised never again to question the voyage.

While Pholos paid no heed to Jason's claim that the voyage was real, he stopped discussing the matter for the sake of having peace in the house. Jason, however, frequently discussed the story-game with his friends and somehow persuaded them that Argo was real and that the voyage was fact. Pholos surmised, and I felt compelled to agree, that Jason was able to convince his playmates because they realized that he truly believed that what he said was true. By the time Jason left Pelion, most of the younger folk on the mountain had accepted as fact that the Argonauts had been to Kolchis and returned with a golden fleece.

Now this was odd—Jason's convincing his friends that he had sailed to Kolchis at the same time as when he was living among them. How could his friends, boys his own age, believe what couldn't possibly be true? Yet if Jason could convince friends who knew better, it stands to reason that he would find it equally easy to persuade strangers that the story-game was true. And since the Argo game was more or less realistically designed, and rowing a ship to Kolchis was not impossible, a well-delivered presentation of the Argonautika may well be accepted as true. Thinking such thoughts, a rush of misgivings flooded my brain: I cursed myself and Krorones for misleading Jason's mind. The game had become Jason's reality because he had experienced it as such. When Jason told others about the story-game, he wasn't telling a lie. He was merely recounting what his mind had experienced as fact.

Within a short dozen years, Jason's story had become history, spreading first through Thessaly, then south to Korinthos, and quickly to the rest of Hellas. The merchants of Korinthos jumped on the chance to trade with the countries ringing the Euxine Sea. Based on Jason's account, Korinthos built galleys that were super fast to evade the Trojan navy guarding the Hellespont, and sufficiently strong to handle the dangerous waters of the Euxine Sea. The shipbuilding program was sponsored by Atreus, king of Mycenae and overlord of Korinthos, whose palace-run economy had trouble producing enough grain in the dry Argolid plain. Imports of wheat from Skythia and other Euxine lands became a necessity, and as the Hellenes needed ever more food, Trojan control of the Hellespont passage progressed from being a mere nuisance to becoming an existential threat. The tug-of-war between Hellenic ships trying to sail through the Hellespont and the Trojan navy attempting to extract tribute grew more heated with each passing year until Agamemnon, the son and successor of Atreus, formed a coalition of one hundred and sixty-four Hellenic states and made war against Troy. Led by Agamemnon, the Hellenes invaded the Troad four years ago, and since then the two armies have been fighting to a draw in the dusty plain between the Aegean Sea and the heavily walled Trojan citadel.

With the Trojans busy battling the Hellenes, the Helles-pont/Bosporos route is now open to all, and ships are sailing regularly to the Euxine region. Since rowing a ship eastward to Sinope or westward to the Ister's mouth is no longer a nov-elty, few men living today have reason to doubt the veracity of Jason's original tale. Certainly the core of the story-game—sailing from Hellas to Kolchis—is now widely accepted as true, even as each retelling results in a revision or two, and often a whole lot more. The result is that in the thirty years since Jason left for Korinthos, the story has fathered more offsprings than the Lernean hydra had heads.

A good example is the size of the crew and who was or wasn't a member. The story-game had thirty rowers plus Orpheus, the singer, and Tiphys, the helmsman, for a total crew of thirty-two. But as bards retold the story at hundreds of late-night banquets, some claimed that as many as fifty men had rowed the ship, while others insisted that no more than twenty participated. And there's certainly no agreement about the crew's roster. A majority of the Argonauts were Minyan by descent, but certainly not all, and Theseus was not an Argo shipmate no matter how loudly the Athenians insist that he was.

Another false rumor is that the Argonauts got lost on the way back. Jason had reasoned correctly that sailing home wouldn't pose any new problems, but the bards who make their living by singing long ballads keep extending the story because the longer their song, the better their pay. One improbable ver-sion has the Argonauts rowing up the Ister River instead of down the Bosporos. How stupid a notion! How could anyone believe a story like that? Ister is a gigantic river flowing from west to east before merging into the Euxine Sea. Rowing upriver would have taken Jason to Pannonia and hundreds of miles farther west. Incredible as it seems, the rumor mill has the Argonauts doing exactly that and—can you believe it?—finding a way around the snow-covered Alps, sailing down and up Italy, and finally returning to Hellas after dragging the ship across the Libyan desert. Jason's story-game was realistically constructed—except for the first day, when the ship covered too many miles—while the traveling bards' silly additions have no credibility at all.

But if Jason had nothing to do with the bards' invention of a roundabout back voyage, I suspect that he had a hand in Medeia's metamorphosis from beautiful maiden to evil witch. At the end of the story-game, when the Argonauts quit Kolchis and Medeia stayed behind, Jason hadn't yet come to grips with who she really was. He loved her but didn't know her. She was a princess, but there were none on Pelion. Jason was a teenager while Medeia was a grown woman. He thought Medeia was like Chariklo, or vice versa, but he didn't know Chariklo either. So when she and I got married, Jason's vision of Medeia collapsed because she was not who he thought she was. He could no longer love her because he thought she had betrayed him, and he could no longer trust her because he thought she had changed her mind.

In the story-game Jason rationalized that Medeia rejected him and remained in Kolchis because he had inadvertently killed her brother. But Jason didn't believe his own rationale. He regarded the killing as a simple error. He erroneously had thought that Medeia needed protection, and had acted to protect her. He had always been true and loyal to her, and nothing he said or did justified her rejection of him. Her action didn't make sense; it was unjust. No Hellenic woman would have acted the way she did. Didn't Harmonia marry Kadmos, and didn't Hippodameia fall in love with Pelops? If Medeia had been a Hellenic maiden instead of a weird, foreign woman, she never would have rejected him.

Well, Jason wasn't the first lothario, or the last, who would fault the woman for not returning his love. But by calling Medeia *weird*, Jason was serving raw meat to the makers of myths, who lost no time attributing all kinds of heinous crimes to the Kolchian maid. She was accused of witchcraft and sorcery; cutting her brother into pieces; murdering King Peleas, King Kreon, and Jason's wife, Glauke; and, most horrendous of all, killing her two children merely to teach Jason a lesson. The Hellenes are, of course, known for ascribing the worst possible attributes to women who refuse to conform to their ultra-patriarchal norms. Hellenic women are kept uneducated, have few legal rights, and are subordinate to father and husband; in fact they are barely a step above slaves. Medeia wasn't like that; she didn't fit the Hellenic mold but was a *gasan* in her own right, with a will of her own. Her very persona was a threat to the Hellenic social order. So the Hellenic bards, out to please their male patrons, took to demonizing Medeia by calling her foreign, weird, and ultimately evil, just like the mythical Amazons, whom the Hellenes felt justified to kill in order to protect their supposedly exceptional civilization.

Ethnic arrogance has been my people's curse since the time the Minyans conquered Thessaly and forced us to live on Pelion. Different in looks, language, and customs, they called us *barbarians* and treated us with contempt while, ironic as it was, they sent their sons to my school to be taught what only we knew. Unfortunately, if that's the right word, the school's popularity precipitated the destruction of our community. With peace in the region, the Hellenes tried to improve relations between our peoples and invited us to the wedding of Peirithoos and Hippodameia. I had a cold and anyhow didn't want to go, but many of my friends decided to attend. The wedding was an unspeakable horror. The party started out fine; wine was served and music was played, but when the women got up to dance and our men tried to join in, all hell broke loose because, contrary to our tradition, the Hellenes believe that mixed-gender dancing is not only indecent but a serious crime. When Peirithoos accused our men of rape and worse, the Hellenes attacked and killed more than forty of us, decimating our already small clan. Many of my closest friends were killed. Only Nessos managed to escape and, unable to return to his lean-to on the mountain, decided to take a job in Aitolia on the banks of the Euenos River.

A few years after the wedding disaster, Jason's primal nemesis, King Peleas of Iolkos, died to no one's regret. His regency devolved on Admetos of Pherai, whose legitimacy is based on his marriage to Peleas's daughter, Alkestis. This means that Admetos's right to the throne is as contestable as Peleas's claim had been, with Jason posing the same threat to the new king as he had to Peleas fifty years ago. With no useful purpose served by revealing Jason's royal lineage, I buried the secret for good.

Life on Pelion is gradually drifting toward extinction as younger folks leave the mountain, and the old pass away. I continue to run the school with the help of Chariklo and old Krorones, who pitches in whenever he can. It's hard work, but nothing gives me more joy than hearing from former pupils about goings-on in the greater world. They talk a lot about Herakles—mostly nasty tales—and about Medeia, whose stories are equally nasty. I also hear bits and pieces about certain Argonauts, but only occasionally is there news about Jason, and what I do hear makes little sense. They say Jason sailed to Kolchis not once but several times, and became a wealthy merchant, trading armor and pottery for Kolchian gold and iron ore. He is said to have no interest in politics or military affairs; wealth is his only goal. They say that after the death of his wife, Jason succumbed to loneliness and depression, and he often walked to Kenchrai to visit Argo's rotting hull. One day he fell asleep next to his old ship, and a loose plank fell on his head, or so they say. He would have been forty-nine at the time.

But I don't believe any of this. Knowing Jason, I believe he simply took off when Korinthos got boring, eager to meet new people and eager to explore the newly settled islands of Meligunis and Pithecusae in the west.

It took me years to learn to live without Jason. I am here and he is wherever; all we have is remembrance of a shared past. Even now, after all these years, news about the voyage or the shipmates evokes Jason's image as if he had left only yesterday. Visitors come and go, bringing plenty of news and hearsay and also many good stories that fight off the mountain's gloomy mood. Alas most stories are about Herakles, the great celebrity of our time, and all are about his killing whoever crosses his path. Herakles never forgave the Argonauts for abandoning him in Bythnia and exacted revenge at every opportunity, first killing Periklymenos at Pylos, then Erginos at Thebes, Iphitos at Tiryns, and Nessos at Kalydona after ferrying his wife across the Euenos River. The Hellenes, caring little about right and wrong, extol Herakles because he always wins and never loses. His virtue is killing, and since he is the best killer, the Hellenes glorify him—even claim that he is a god. How different we are, my people and the Hellenes. They wept when he died of a painful skin disease while I praised the happy day to heaven's height. Jason had been right to rid his crew of that awful man when fate gave him the chance.

A year or two after Agamemnon invaded Troy, I received the most wonderful visitor of all: King Peleus of Myrmidon, the father of Achilles, my erstwhile charge. As the last of the Argonauts to survive, Peleus was anxious to talk about Jason's voyage, the confrontation in Kolchis, and what he called the taking of the Golden Fleece. Peleus recounted in detail the tragic death of Kyzikos, saying it was his fault, not Jason's, that their friend was slain. Needless to say, Peleus's words threw me for a loop. I was old but I still had my wits, and I knew the real Peleus, the one sitting across from me, had never met the fictional Kyzikos of Jason's story-game. So what was going on? Was Peleus insane, or was he testing me?

But one thing was clear: Peleus was not confused. He believed what he said was true, namely that he had sailed with Jason to Kolchis and brought back the Golden Fleece. Wasn't it just any old gold-speckled fleece? No, Peleus insisted, the fleece was the coat of the ram that had taken Phrixos to Kolchis years before. His words were nonsense, straight from the mythmakers' desks, words describing events that never had happened. I had no wish to quarrel with Peleus; the man was very old, and if he wanted to cling to foolish ideas, it wasn't my job to set him straight. Yet I was too curious to let the matter drop, and gently asked Peleus whether he remembered the date of the voyage. His immediate answer implied that Jason, with Peleus aboard, had sailed to Kolchis ten years after the story-game. That equated to four years after Jason's arrival in Korinthos. What on earth! If Peleus's memory was right, Jason would have been twenty-three at the time of that voyage, not thirteen but a grown-up man flourishing in the seafaring capital of the world.

Not wishing to reveal my surprise, I quickly switched subjects and asked Peleus about the Trojan War. At the time it was going back and forth, with neither side gaining on the other. The Trojans were ensconced in their citadel and controlled the Mysian hinterland while the Hellenic army occupied the Plain of Ilion and conducted raids up and down the Anatolian coast. Agamemnon was commander in chief of the Hellenic forces because his one hundred ships, together with his brother's sixty, were the largest component of the Hellenic alliance. Peleus confirmed he'd contributed fifty ships, each carrying one hundred and twenty Mirmydons under Achilles's command. The Iolkos/Pherai contingent of eleven ships was led by King Eumelos, who had succeeded his father, Admetos.

Peleus contended the war was both necessary and just in order to secure free access to the Euxine Sea. Trade was to everyone's benefit, and no one had the right to blockade the Hellespont. The Trojans were scum, and progress was impossible as long as they held sway. Peleus conceded that before the Argonautika, no one had known of the wealth of the Euxine lands, but once everyone did, conflict had become inevitable. Did he mean Jason's voyage had been the cause of the Trojan War? No, of course not! The Kyzikos fiasco had left a deep mark in Jason's heart, making him a peaceful man, unwilling to start any war, least of all against Troy. But yes, it was also true that without Jason's voyage there may never have been a Trojan War.

So wherein lies the truth? I know for a fact that Jason played his story-game when he was thirteen years old. The story-game was fiction that simulated an imagined reality, giving the game its credibility and paving the way for its ultimate acceptance as truth. But what about Jason? Did he know the difference between playing the game and experiencing the real thing? For the longest time I wasn't sure of the workings of his mind, but Peleus's account of his voyage seems to explain what I had missed: Jason, it seems, had made not one but two trips, the first in his mind, the second in reality.

The story-game began as therapy but became a plan Jason was eager to execute as soon as he could. The merchants of Korinthos gave him the means, and off he sailed to Kolchis, the first Hellene to traverse the Euxine Sea. Jason would have experienced both trips, first by constructing the story-game and later by actually making the voyage. The story got around first, with Jason swearing it was fact, and when his audiences accepted the story as real, there was every reason to repeat the event. No one would have expected the second voyage, which in reality was the first, to turn out exactly as described in the game as long as the ship passed through the Bosporos and ended up at the Phasis River.

Is this how it happened? Did Jason ultimately realize his boyhood dream by piloting a real ship to the Euxine Sea? It's certainly a beautiful notion, and one that fits all the facts, yet no one living today can verify both of its parts. Peleus is a case in point. Having heard about the story-game voyage, he may have joined Jason on the second trip without realizing it was really the first. Chariklo's recollection is limited to the time Jason developed the story-game, but like me she never saw him again after he left Pelion. So what can we know? Theories aren't proof, and there's no way to prove mine. What's certain is that Jason was my adopted son, that he invented a daring adventure, and that shortly thereafter a Hellenic ship, possibly captained by Jason, sailed from Hellas to Kolchis for the very first time.

Medeia, however, was never a riddle—not to me, not to Krorones and Nessos, and certainly not to Jason. Medeia was not an invention; she was real. Medeia was always Chariklo, and Chariklo was always Medeia; they were one and the same, a beautiful young woman who was loved by all but had only one heart to give. As I am telling you my story, Chariklo is roasting a piglet I trapped this morning on my exercise walk. She is as bewitchingly beautiful as she was on our wedding day sixty-five years ago. And if you don't believe me, ask for Cheiron's cave on Pelion and join us for supper as the mountain's pale dusk closes the day.

ARGONAUTIKA

Place Names
1 Aietes Palace
2 Canastra
3 Gyropolis
4 Abydos
5 Mastusia
6 Aphetae
7 Aianteion
8 Iolkos
9 Athena
10 Korinthos
11 Pisa
12 Troy
13 Cape Carambis
14 Sinopi
15 Themiskyra
16 Kolchis

SKYTHIA

THRAKI

Bodies of Water
A Pagasai Bay
B Aegean Sea
C Bay of Meleas
D Hellespont
E Propontis
F Bosporos

SKYTHIA

Euxine Sea

KOLCHIS

NATOLIA

Rivers
U Ister
V Amyrus
W Rhebas
X Phasis
Y Halys
Z Thermodon

Islands
20 Pelion
21 Pallene
22 Athos
23 Lemnos
24 Imbros
25 Samothraki
26 Tenedos
27 Chersonisos
28 Arctonisos
29 Clashing Rocks
30 Skiathos
31 Thynias
32 Ares

Other novels by Wolfgang Schoellkopf

Two Thousand Eighty-Four

Rainbows

Julia in Hellas

New York Measure